Lone Star Lodge
Lodge Trail
Hangover Hedge
Gwendolyn Lane
The Woodshed

Praise for

Loodor Tales

"*The Land of the Pines* should engage children and adults alike. Our quest for the meaning of life is a constant journey, and Loodor Tales shows this is ever-evolving for each of us. These tales encourage all of us to take a moment every day to pause and look around. Notice something you didn't see the day prior. And also look inside yourself if you want a different outcome. Our souls reflect the most honest versions of who we are."

—Jennifer Levene Bruno
Vice President, Group Publishing Director,
Elle Decor, House Beautiful, Town & Country, Veranda

"Such a sweet and compelling story conveying wonderful insights about character, kindness, and positivity. I totally enjoyed it, couldn't put it down once I started; I was captivated by Grey's journey to learn the power of her voice."

—Debbie Storey
President & CEO,
AT&T Performing Arts Center

"The author's very original story and vivid characters bring the whole world to life in a magical way. Underneath all the playful prose, she makes many insightful comments."

—Sandra Campos
Fashion CEO, Founder of Fashion Launchpad

"A delightful story of a darling kitten's journey to learn the importance of friendship, forgiveness, and fortitude told through an endearing menagerie, a couple pine trees, and assorted barn furniture."

—Dr. Luci Higgins
Superintendent of Schools,
Cornerstone Christian Schools

"This book contains many examples that young people can learn from as they grow up. A compelling story that offers very natural entertainment and a strong finish."

—Markham Benn Sr.
Vice President, IBC Bank,
Board Member of San Antonio Youth Literacy

"What a book!"

—Rene Salinas
Chief of Security,
Alamo Rangers

"An inspiring book with powerful messages presented in a unique way that is as important for adults as it is for children."

—Gary D. Compton,

Vice President to Energy Industry Icon
and Philanthropist T. Boone Pickens;
Chairman of the Texas Youth Commission
under Governors Bill Clements,
Ann Richards, and George W. Bush

"A classic in the making, *The Land of the Pines* introduces a stellar new literary talent. Nilsson's ability to deftly tackle complex issues in such a format makes this a rewarding and enlightening read, no matter your age."

—Naomi Rougeau,

Senior Fashion Features Editor,
ELLE

"What an inspiration to all generations on the lessons of life. The illustrations are exquisite and impart the sensitivity with which the story was crafted. This is a dream come true and a keepsake forever!"

—Kate Kelly Smith,

EVP Managing Director,
Luxe Interiors + Design

"One debut you don't want to miss. *The Land of the Pines* is the ideal read for all ages from child to adult with lessons in kindness and friendship, and characters that shine on the page."

—Readers' Favorite

loodur tales

THE LAND of the PINES

SUMMER NILSSON

This is a work of fiction. Any similarity to real persons, living or dead, is coincidental and not intended by the author.

Loodor Tales: The Land of the Pines

Printed in the United States of America
10 9 8 7 6 5 4 3 2 1

Published by Loodor Publishing
Dallas, Texas

For more information or to contact the author, please visit www.loodor.com.

Cover design, interior design, and composition by Loodor Publishing

Library of Congress Control Number: 2021907804

Publisher's Cataloging-in-Publication data is available.

Print ISBN: 978-1-954401-00-6

eBook ISBN: 978-1-954401-01-3

Distributed by Greenleaf Book Group

For ordering information, please contact Greenleaf Book Group at PO Box 91869, Austin, TX 78709, 512.891.6100.

Dedicated to my nieces and nephew:
You are the product of your own creation.

Dedication

With Friday lights aglow and all the town to know,
The crowning nod of credit aside,
In search of all the mass, I ran at dawn's first pass
Looking for myself in someone's eyes.

And what I wish I'd known
Through all the years I've grown:
What you find within is all that counts.

So, when the car drives east and my mind's at rest,
It's here I know I'm at my very best.

Living through your laugh, while studying your craft,
I see the world at play and it's okay.
So cautious to achieve, a winner's web to weave,
I'm offering the view I didn't have.

And what I wish you'd see,
The many things you'll be,
The world is yours to take if you'll just grab.

So, when you smile that smile, all I feel is blessed,
For I know one day you'll also head out west.

Contents

Prologue

Special Report

Laura saw the glow of the red light as it counted down. She knew that it was time.

"Thank you for joining me. I'm Laura, Special Reporter for *The Buzzy Bark.* We're live from Black Mountain Farm, where we've worked behind the scenes to bring you an exclusive story. In this story, new heroes rise to meet great expectations. Friends become foes and vice versa. We're reminded that one moment can change everything, including an animal's station.

"Stay tuned as we take you inside this never-before-told tale."

Chapter One

The Pine Family

Mrs. Pine watched as her family held hands and swayed back and forth. She could hear the younger trees whispering to each other.

"Do you see it? Look at those long legs."

"The stripes make it look like a tiger, and those blue eyes . . . they're the color of the sky."

"What should we call it?"

Mrs. Pine laughed to herself. She loved the saplings' energy. She'd watched many trees grow up to become steady, strong members of the Pine family. Mrs. Pine took great pride in being their mother. She stood as the tallest and oldest tree in the family, as well as on the mountain. Her husband, Mr. Pine, was exactly three minutes younger and three inches shorter than she. He'd stood next to her from day one, albeit shorter. She often liked to remind him of that.

As she heard her family debate different names for the newborn in the valley below, Mrs. Pine wrote its birth announcement for *The Buzzy Bark*, the official news source on the farm. The Pine family loved sharing the news on the farm each week, so they created *The Buzzy Bark.* Mrs. Pine made sure that her reporters always published the truth. The farm animals appreciated and trusted her honesty. She shared stories and events as soon as they happened on the farm, and she felt it was her duty to remain fair on all things.

"Let it be known that today is a special day, with the flowers in bloom, the butterflies aflutter, and the robins singing their celebratory tune. Today, a beautiful kitten was born in the Jam Barn of Black Mountain Farm," Mrs. Pine read aloud. She wanted to hear how her words sounded in case she needed to edit them.

"Wait," said Mr. Pine. "We need to give this cat a proper name. It is more than just 'a beautiful kitten.' We have the chance to set it on the right path. We need to give it an identity."

Mrs. Pine agreed that the cat needed an actual name. She thought about it. She wanted to give the kitten a name that fit. The name "Grey" seemed powerful. The kitten's gray fur, with its black- and sand-colored stripes, was spectacular. It would likely become known for these special stripes and markings. Mrs. Pine could play off the kitten's bright white feet, but the name "Socks" just didn't seem to fit this cat.

"We'll call the kitten Grey," Mrs. Pine declared. "It's a strong name that will open any door. This name will guarantee that other animals will take this cat seriously." The other trees swayed in agreement. "Now, that covers the name. We can't confirm anything else. One's identity is defined by their character."

Mrs. Pine shared the official news about Grey with the Beehive News Distribution Team. She gave the bees clear instructions: "Spread the story to the farm community as quickly as possible." Mrs. Pine knew the news about the vulnerable kitten would move all over the mountain. She needed the strongest blue jay to protect Grey.

Mrs. Pine called Laura, Special Reporter for *The Buzzy Bark*. She said, "Make sure Miss Jay the Bird is the first one to know about Grey. Tell her that she will need to step up as Grey's guardian. We believe that this is a special cat, but it will need help finding its voice. Knowing Miss Jay, it's bound to become a singing voice. That's all we can share at this time."

That really was all I could share, Mrs. Pine thought to herself once Laura had left. She had to keep Grey's destiny close to the vest for now. Timing was everything.

Mrs. Pine watched Laura and the other bees take off. Rain or shine, the bees never missed a delivery. They made sure to prioritize important stories. With the directives in place by the pines and powers that be, the farm was abuzz with the breaking news about a new, special kitten.

One's identity
is defined by
their character.

2

Chapter Two
Easy on the Growl

Grey knew she and her siblings were born minutes apart in the same barn. They had the same mom. There was no way around the fact that they were related. She just wasn't sure how that was possible. Bob, her brother, was all boy. He was born without a tail, but what he lacked in a tail he made up for with a fiery temperament. It was like their mom knew that a tail would just weigh him down. Bob was fearless, but he played rough: way too rough for Grey. They had a sister named Shi. Shi only talked to Bob, never to Grey. Bob always acted so different around Shi. He was calm and protective. Grey couldn't understand why he always shielded Shi, and Grey never knew why the three of them could never play together. Two was company, and three was a crowd.

The bond between her siblings didn't bother Grey because she had made a friend. Her new friend took care of her. Bob and Shi thought her friend was funny. Or weird. Maybe they thought the friendship itself was weird. Grey didn't really know what she had done to deserve this new friend, but she knew that life sure was better when you had someone to talk to.

Their mom returned to the woods a few weeks after they were born. She'd explained that some animals just weren't meant to live in barns, and she was one of them. Within a few days, Bob and Shi announced that they planned to join her someday. They started acting strange. They would stand on ledges in the barn and growl with rough, deep voices. Grey didn't get it, but she had a feeling it meant they were leaving soon. Maybe they were trying to send their mom a message.

Grey wondered if Bob and Shi would judge her if

she didn't follow them to the woods. She had started to feel a strange, new desire. Grey didn't want them to judge her; she wanted them to like her. Even if they did judge her, though, Grey knew she wanted to stay here. It almost felt like she *had* to stay here . . . wherever here was.

3

Chapter Three

Black Mountain Farm

Mr. Joe and Miss B owned Black Mountain Farm, or BMF. BMF was made of two parts: the farm and the mountain. Both sections offered totally different experiences. In contrast to the clean and organized farm below, the elevated "mountain" was covered in wild shrubs and fields of flowers that miraculously grew in the red ore dirt. Many believed the bright soil had special powers because of all that grew there. Mr. Joe and Miss B created walking trails on and around the mountain. They worked hard to maintain the trails so they could enjoy the wildlife of the area.

Mr. Joe had personally mapped out each walking trail. He had thought about the direction of the sun and where it would shine throughout the day. Mr. Joe's long hikes in the morning always began in the east. He greeted the pine trees with a nod of gratitude for their many years of service. Some days, he was almost sure that he could hear them respond.

Mr. Joe then made his way to the lake. As a gift to Miss B, he had placed park benches by the water so they could have picnics on pretty days. Those little moments were very important to Miss B, and she was always touched when Mr. Joe made the extra effort. On his solo walks, Mr. Joe enjoyed sitting on a bench and feeding the fish in the lake. They always jumped out of the water and splashed around to welcome him.

The west side of the mountain provided an entirely different view. On some days, Mr. Joe could hike to the highest elevation on the mountain. He enjoyed a view of untouched trees that extended for miles and miles. This was the perfect spot for watching sunsets, which he loved to do with Miss B. They watched in awe as the sky shifted from shades of electric pink to orange.

At the bottom of the mountain, the husband and wife worked together as a team. They each completed different tasks on the farm. They lived in a white 1850s farmhouse that they had worked hard to update. Their favorite addition was a screened-in porch that wrapped around the house. This porch was the perfect spot to sit under the fans, drink iced tea, and watch the birds.

Over the years, Miss B had transformed BMF into a farm-to-table tourist attraction. Guests from the city could rent one of the BMF log cabins on their weekend trips or take a cooking class with Miss B. Miss B also took care of the farm's fruit orchards, from which she made delicious jams. Everyone wanted Miss B's treasured jams when she sold them each spring.

Mr. Joe kept a watchful eye on his prized vegetable gardens, where he grew tomatoes, peppers, and squash. He also maintained the farm's beautiful landscape. Mr. Joe was an early riser; he was always up with the chickens. He could be found working on odd jobs after the sun went down. Mr. Joe worked harder than anyone he knew, and he was very proud of his attention to detail. At dinnertime, Miss B would often walk out onto the porch and yell, "Get it while it's hot!" with a smile, knowing that Mr. Joe would be late to the table again. Both Mr. Joe and Miss B found great joy in a long day's work.

"Have you seen the new gray kitten in the Jam Barn?" an excited Miss B asked over dinner. "It's precious. It let me pick it right up. It just laid there in my arms, purring. It has the most beautiful blue eyes I've ever seen."

Mr. Joe knew where this was going, and he would have none of it. "Don't think for one second that you're bringing that cat into this house," he barked. "These farm cats are meant to live into the barn and help with the mice. That's their only role: they're working cats. This one *might* be as cute as can be, but it's still staying in the barn. It'll just be happy to have a safe spot to sleep. After all, there's a natural order to things. It's important that everyone has a place. To be clear, that cat's place is in the barn."

Miss B was a total mush. She'd let every new kitten on the farm live in the house if she could. While Mr. Joe loved her compassion, he knew that he had to be the voice of reason. He could tell from his wife's grin that, while he may have won the discussion for today, this new kitten would be the best-fed barn cat at BMF.

As they enjoyed dinner and talked about their day, neither of them noticed the blue jay listening intently from the dining room windowsill.

4

Chapter Four
The Spider's Sweet Tooth

The spider didn't remember much about her first days. She'd been kept snug in a warm, silky bubble with her brothers and sisters for what felt like years. At first, it was oddly comfortable. As the days dragged on, though, the bubble grew dark and crowded. The spiders all seemed to slam into each other. They grew impatient, waiting for their freedom.

What a crazy day that was: her "birthday," of sorts. The bubble burst, and the sudden light blinded her. Mass chaos ensued. She quickly realized that she was smaller than everyone else because they trampled all over her. As the last of her siblings ran away, she picked herself up and followed. They all scattered in different directions. For reasons unknown to her, they ran out of the room. None of the little spiders knew where to go. They just put their heads down and dashed, their little legs moving as fast as they could.

The spider was exhausted. She felt like she'd been running for hours. She was breathing heavily, so she smelled it long before she saw it. She didn't know what the sweet smell was or how to describe the way it made her feel. Her stomach suddenly made a deep moaning sound. As she got closer to the smell, her body began to tremble. The wind in the trees tried to blow her back, but she dug her feet into the ground and pushed forward. She was determined to follow that sweet scent.

The spider was in awe of what she saw. She walked up to a building very different from the one she had left. This building was white. Bright pink flowers grew up the sides. Two rose-patterned rocking chairs sat outside, clearly enjoying the day. She could see birds watching from their nests in the trees above. Metal ornaments guarded the front entrance. As she walked closer, she noticed that the first building matched a much larger white one further down the path.

The spider spotted a tiny crack along the back of the first white building. She knew she was small enough to squeeze through. She darted away from the other spiders and crept through the crack. She immediately knew that this wasn't any old building: it was a labor of love. Row upon row of shiny silver tables stood neatly end to end, each covered with a pale yellow checkered cloth and perfectly positioned glass jars. The jars were all different colors, each of them labeled. In the middle of the room, a delicate old desk dozed peacefully. On that desk were stacks of brown bags, a pen, and a journal. There was so much to take in. The spider started to feel weak.

That's when she saw what she had smelled: the sweet smell came from a peach-colored spot on the floor. She could see it clearly because the rest of the space was so clean and purposeful. She felt a sudden push on her back, as though something was shoving her forward to investigate. She moved with a new energy to feed her growling belly. She touched the peach-colored spot with her front leg. It was a sticky, liquidy goo. It smelled delicious. She couldn't stand it any longer. She brought the goo to her mouth and tasted it. She heard a voice the instant she swallowed:

"You think that tastes good? Wait till you've tasted power."

Peach
PEACHES
Peach

5

Chapter Five
The Harrowing Hourglass

The spider felt like an enormous lightning bolt had shocked her and taken over her entire body. A red glow fell over the floor. It was strange; that red light hadn't been there before. She looked down at herself. It appeared that the light came from her body. The spider was very confused.

"Who's there? What is this? What's happening?"

she asked, not sure who she was talking to. Was she talking to herself? Was she crazy?

The red light had appeared as soon as the sweet, sticky goo hit her lips. The sweet goo seemed to feed the red light, not her. Then she heard something.

"Some might call me a magic wand," a voice emerged. "I find that cute. I'm so much more than a wand. Many spiders have marks on their stomach. I appear on your back so that we're guaranteed to overshadow others. Do you see our glow in your reflection on the desk? That's me—or, rather, us. I function as your timekeeper, beating to the drum of our deepest desires. Let's call this our twitching hour, for kicks. That tremble you felt awakens me so I can light the way and get things done. One might say that I feed the chatter and dialogue in that mind of yours. We're a team, you and I. We'll help each other. The other animals will find me harrowing. You shouldn't. I'm your Hourglass."

The spider thought of the sweet goo. She still didn't quite understand why the Hourglass was here. "So, you show up when I'm hungry?"

"Yes . . . and no," the Hourglass replied. "What are you really hungry for? You're a Black Widow. You don't know what that means yet, but that's okay. I'm here to show you. You'll learn that we don't want what the other animals want. We don't crave friendship. We crave control. That's where I step in. I release our potential.

"Not a lot of animals will resist us. That's the real sweet spot—where the rubber meets the road. Some animals actually *want* to be controlled. Not many are strong enough to walk their own path and defy the odds. They'll quickly learn that there just isn't enough room on the path for resistance."

The Harrowing Hourglass shot a red beam of light at a jar on the bottom shelf. The jar shattered into a thousand tiny pieces. The Hourglass loved to destroy things. Glass and goo covered the floor, and the Widow ate in silence until her stomach hurt. She couldn't stop herself. As she ate, the Widow watched the red glow of the Hourglass illuminate them in the dark.

6

Chapter Six
Flower Power

Growing up, Miss Jay never stayed in one place for too long. Her family flew around from farm to farm. Miss Jay rarely had a chance to get to know any of the other young birds. By the time she made a new friend, her family moved to the next community.

Everywhere she went, animals were always in awe of Miss Jay's feathers. She looked like she wore a blue cape over her bright white chest. She was particularly proud of the stripes on her tail. Miss Jay wore a crown of soft feathers on her head. Those head feathers rose up when she was in a mood. She was a very expressive bird, and she didn't hide her feelings when other birds wasted her time.

One good thing about traveling so much was that Miss Jay met many different types of animals. She met poets, medics, and musicians. Miss Jay liked the doctors and nurses the most. She tried to learn as much as she could from them. After watching them work, Miss Jay knew her calling was to become a caregiver. Taking care of others felt so natural to her. So did the sing-alongs. Miss Jay found that she was very gifted with music. She learned that she could pick up just about any instrument and play along with the other musicians she met. Her favorite instrument by far was the banjo.

Like many drifters, Miss Jay and her parents didn't own many things. Her mom suggested that Miss Jay start making jewelry out of the fresh flowers they found on each farm.

Making jewelry would keep Miss Jay busy and still feed her creative spirit.

No matter where she went, Miss Jay made friends with the flowers. They loved the attention. The flowers encouraged Miss Jay to find a place to stay for good. They taught her that a home was so much more than a nest to sleep in. The wildflowers pushed Miss Jay to try to make friends with everyone she met.

One wildflower friend explained it best: "Look, we're all in this together. Everyone contributes to this life in their own special way. The flowers bloom for everyone's success. We know that how we speak to one another makes all the difference."

Miss Jay began to approach the weeks of travel differently. She looked forward to discovering a new spot. After all, that new place could be "the one." She was on a mission to plant her own roots, to find a community she could protect and help grow. Miss Jay would look back on this mission one day and lovingly call it her "Flower Power."

7

Chapter Seven
Grey & Her Guardian

Grey learned early on that there were few things as beautiful as a spring morning on the farm. It was her favorite part of the day.

Each morning, the sun greeted Grey with a smile, slowly lighting the sky with enough energy for the day. Grey could feel the sun's warmth and dedication as it moved from one side of the sky to the other, dawn to dusk. The sun marked the hours of the day like a guide-post from above.

Her brother and sister planned to leave any day. Grey was still confused about their desire to leave. She was even a little sad. However, Grey knew she was a lucky cat. She had Miss Jay. Miss Jay remained resolutely by Grey's side as her new friend and guardian.

Miss Jay explained that, as Grey's guardian, her job was to look after Grey. When Grey was born, Mrs. Pine had sent word through the bees that Grey was Miss Jay's new responsibility. Grey was glad that Miss Jay had her back. She had heard that the blue jay was a force to be reckoned with. It must have been true; Grey noticed that no one messed with them.

Grey also noticed that Miss Jay always knew when other animals needed attention. Everyone felt at peace around the bird. They respected Miss Jay for her brilliant mind, but they loved her heart even more. She was funny and warm. Miss Jay was also artsy and unique, with a bohemian flair. She always wore stacks of bracelets and decorated her beautiful nest with colorful notes that said "Better Barn Vibes" and "Boss Bird."

Miss Jay watched as Grey talked to the other animals on the farm. Grey had a talent for reading other animals in seconds. She knew when to speak. More importantly, Grey knew when to stay quiet. Miss Jay often praised Grey for this skill. She told Grey that this instinct couldn't be taught. Grey was calculated and precise. Miss Jay explained that these traits could be both a gift and a curse.

Grey knew she was a beautiful cat. Still, she thought her stripes distracted from who she really was. She worried that the other animals thought her markings were too much. Grey thought that it must be easier for others to dislike her, even though she tried very hard to be likeable. Miss Jay tried to teach Grey not to take herself so seriously.

"There's a big difference between laughing at yourself and diminishing your self-worth," Miss Jay noted. "You'll drive yourself crazy trying to be perfect. Instead, you should celebrate what makes you different. Those long legs will help you reach heights that most animals can't even dream about. Laugh when you fall down. Then, pick yourself up and dust yourself off. You know full well that you're just getting started."

Grey soaked up Miss Jay's encouragement like a sponge. She was still confused about one thing, though.

"I don't understand why Bob and Shi run away from Miss B," she asked. "I love playing with Miss B and her guests. I could do it all day every day. I want more attention, but Bob and Shi want less. Why is that?"

Miss Jay knew the answer could get complicated, especially if Grey wanted more attention later on. She offered the following insight for now: "Not all animals are cut out for human relationships. Your mom wasn't, and your brother and sister aren't. There's nothing wrong with that. You like human relationships. You may even find a human one day that you feel you were destined to meet. It's really special when that happens. You never know who it could be. You never know the role someone might have in your life.

"Just treat everyone with respect," Miss Jay said with a nod. "The most powerful person in the room is often the one you least expect."

Celebrate what makes you different.

8

Chapter Eight
Permission Denied

The Widow decided to let the Hourglass make all the big decisions. The Hourglass gave her courage and pushed her when it thought she was weak. It encouraged her to build a web in the back of what she soon learned was the Jam Barn. The Widow took great pride in her web. She spent most days just sitting at its center, watching the world around her.

Miss B came to the Jam Barn every morning at 7:00 a.m. She hummed as she walked in, holding a cup of coffee. Miss B carefully placed the mug on Woodie, her delicate desk.

The Widow had learned that Woodie and the rocking chairs outside the Jam Barn had been passed down to Miss B from her grandmother. They were Miss B's prized possessions.

Woodie was hand-painted with flower petals that ran up and down her legs. The petals made sure to tickle her at least once a day. Woodie opened up to reveal a hidden drawer and a mirror. Miss B used the mirror to apply her lipstick after drinking her coffee. The paint on top of Woodie had chipped over the years. One could argue that she had seen better days, but she had an undeniable vintage charm. She usually napped in the afternoons. She was exhausted from her mornings with Miss B, who handwrote the labels for each jar of jam.

The jams had different names: Precious Peach, Strawberry Swirl, Midnight Berry, and Blue Skies. Miss B loved naming her jams; they reminded her of nail polish names. Miss B kept a few "special" jars in the back of the Jam Barn for close friends and guests. Mango Moonshine was the guests' favorite flavor: it was always selling out.

The Widow liked the Jam Barn more and more every day. Even though the Hourglass warned against it, the Widow felt a connection with Miss B. They both hated cockroaches. The Widow took it upon herself to remove the unsightly creatures. Now those gross bugs couldn't contaminate the jams. The Hourglass felt that they should be rewarded for their help around the barn. The other animals did not agree.

The birds watched the Widow from their nests.

"There's an agreement among the residents here," the robins commented to the blue jays.

"Yes, and it's to avoid situations just like this one," the blue jays confirmed. "The rules of the barn are clear. We live by an honor code. We don't take things into our own hands, so to speak. The Widow doesn't seem to care about our code."

The Widow scoffed as she heard the birds gossiping. "We don't ask for permission," she said with confidence. The Hourglass beamed brightly. Just then, a nosy bird flew in for her weekly visit with Woodie. The Widow and the Hourglass watched as the bird sat next to the old desk. The Widow and the Hourglass knew that bird was trouble.

9

Chapter Nine
Double Dare

"We can't be too careful here," the bird advised the desk in a hushed whisper. "It started with the cockroaches. Now she's onto the grasshoppers . . . she's pulling them apart. The ants are terrified. If this were about survival, I'm sure we could all understand . . . but it's not about survival. The Widow wants every animal to know that she will take what she wants when she wants it. She isn't looking for food; she's looking for dominance. The Hourglass studies all of us, just waiting to pounce when the time is right. It's just daring someone to cross them."

Woodie let out a deep sigh and whispered, "Sometimes, I crack open at night to let the mirror peek out." The mirror nodded, as if divulging a deeply guarded secret.

"We can see them plotting," the mirror confirmed. "We need to make a move, before it's too late."

The bird nodded in agreement. "I have an idea on how to keep everyone safe. Let me get to work."

10

Chapter Ten
When the Ants Go Marching In

The ants met with the bluebird in the nest to discuss the plan. They understood their role. They weren't very excited about it, but they knew they were the best fit for the job. The ants also knew that, in Miss B's eyes, they were only one step up from the cockroaches. She always tried to destroy them each spring. The ants survived year after year by being stealthy. They kept their mounds hidden in the corners of the barn. They were easy enough to move with a moment's notice.

"Even if we avoid Miss B's powder traps, we know the Widow will soon be after us," the ants confirmed. "Did you see what she did to the poor grasshoppers? They never saw it coming. Either we follow through with this plan or we get picked apart."

No one wanted to end up like the grasshoppers.

"We keep a schedule because we know schedules work," the ants continued. "We finish our work before Miss B arrives in the morning. We grab leftover scraps and then get out of sight. Tomorrow, we'll get a late start. All the other animals will think we overslept. We'll form a line from Woodie to the Widow, leading Miss B straight to the web. She'll freak out when she finds the spider and she'll forget all about us. When Miss B is focused on driving the Widow out, we'll relocate our mound." The ants looked around at each other, nodding. "This plan has to move fast if we want it to work. We'll need everyone's help."

Hours later, the ants were running late, and well before dawn, they gathered to march. They knew the stakes were high. They slowly made their way toward Woodie, who stayed "asleep" for her part of the master plan. The ants pretended to find a scrap of food and worked together to carry it. They could see the Widow and the Hourglass looking on as they slowly formed a line.

The ants watched as Miss B entered the Jam Barn and greeted a sleepy Woodie with a warm smile. The ants knew Miss B spotted them as soon as she put down her coffee. They all closed their eyes, hoping that whatever happened next would hurt less if they didn't see it coming. The ants were later informed that Miss B followed their trail, hoping they'd lead her straight to their mound. However, that wasn't their plan.

Miss B screamed the second she saw the Widow. The Widow stared straight back at her while the Hourglass beamed with red light.

Chapter Eleven
Yellow

Grey was still sprawled out on her blanket when she heard Miss Jay. She knew it would be a long day. Fun, but long. Grey yawned and got up with a big stretch.

"Rise and shine!" Miss Jay laughed at the lazy cat. "It's time to make the rounds, shake hands, and kiss babies."

Grey and Miss Jay started every Wednesday with a visit to the loyal and loving wildflowers. They made Miss Jay very happy. Grey was sleepy, but she knew it was important to Miss Jay that she appreciated these "fields of gold." Miss Jay flew to the middle of the wildflower patch when they arrived. She called this spot the center of the universe. She had a standing date every Wednesday.

By the time Grey reached Miss Jay's happy place, Miss Jay was almost finished with that week's necklace. The bird wore a yellow chain necklace all week. She came to this field every Wednesday to make a new one. Grey sat and watched as Miss Jay listened to the flowers' stories and laughed at their shared jokes.

After visiting the wildflowers, Grey followed Miss Jay to see Eloise and Emma Rocker. The farm animals lovingly called the pair of rocking chairs the Rocker Sisters. Miss B often joined the sisters. She loved to sit outside on pretty afternoons and greet guests. The sisters were important, and they knew it.

The sisters were each painted differently. The farm animals joked that the chairs' personalities matched their paint. Eloise was soft and calm. Delicate, blush-colored rose petals framed her pretty face. Emma, on the other hand, had a temper. She had thorny red roses on her seat. Eloise and Emma bantered back and forth constantly. They were the same age, equally old, having both been handed down by Miss B's grandmother. At this point, they didn't care about being "appropriate" or polite. The Rocker Sisters talked about everyone. Nothing was off limits, and their position in front of the Jam Barn meant they saw it all. They knew everything that happened on the farm. Grey adored them.

Grey saw a look cross over Miss Jay's face as they both smelled something foul. "What is that?" Grey gagged, coughing. She gagged again. The smell was horrible.

"You think this is bad? You should've been here last night!" Emma reported, clearly annoyed. "A couple of young skunks went out on a date. He moved in for a kiss to wrap up the night. She sprayed him up and down. It's all over the front porch. We're all still working through it. Just look at the poor ornaments."

Grey looked up. The metal ornaments hanging on each side of the front door looked very tired, indeed. She laughed, grateful that Miss Jay was moving on. Grey was just about to step inside the barn when she spotted the snake. Grey did a double take. She leapt into a super-fast backflip off the porch. She then made an award-worthy bounce-off-the-wall landing. Had she not been scared to death by the snake, she would have been amazed at that move.

She heard Miss Jay laughing. "Have you not met Friendly?"

The green grass snake dipped his head in greeting.

Great, Grey thought to herself. *Now I'm the story on the porch.* She could just hear the Rockers. Maybe they'd talk more about the backflip landing than the Friendly freak-out.

"You CAN see that I'm green, right?" teased Friendly. "Have you met a lot of s-s-scary *green* animals on the farm? Don't get me wrong: that was one heck of a flip. I'm s-s-super impressed. But s-s-save it for the red s-s-snakes. They don't mes-s-s around. Even *I* run from the reds-s-s."

Miss Jay was still laughing as they entered the barn. "At some point you'll learn. We may not look alike. We may not even look like we can coexist. But we absolutely can, and we do. Birds, snakes, cats, dogs, frogs, flowers . . . everything. Don't let anyone tell you differently."

Grey knew that Miss Jay believed every animal was just striving to be a yellow wildflower on its best day. This was Miss Jay's gold standard of acceptance. Grey and Miss Jay always finished their daily walk with a visit to Woodie, since they had to wait until she woke from her nap. Woodie told them the real "back of the barn" scoop.

"Here's what I heard," Woodie began. "There's a strange feeling on the mountain. No one can quite put their paw on it. Or their foot. You know what I mean. It's like that thickness in the air that you feel before a big storm. Have you noticed the song dogs quit singing?"

"Yes, I have," Miss Jay confirmed. "What does everyone think it is?"

"Well, it's a theory," Woodie continued. "We all know the coyotes howl when they feel threatened. What if someone has either silenced them or made them feel safe? Same with the foxes; no one can hear them anymore. Is it possible that someone is making friends with the mountain foes?"

Grey watched as Woodie gave Miss Jay a sideways glance. 'Who are the foes?' Grey wondered silently.

Chapter Twelve

The Space Between

Grey watched as Bob and Shi left the Jam Barn for good. The sun was setting. It looked like Bob and Shi chased the changing colors as they ran off into the horizon. Perhaps even the orange sky itself was symbolic of a shift. Their leaving hadn't been a surprise. Bob had even asked Grey to join them, but she said no. As certain as Grey had been in that moment, she was now nervous. She silently wondered if staying behind made Bob, Shi, and their mom disappointed in her. Grey really wanted to make them proud. She just didn't know how.

Before Bob left, he turned to Grey and said something that stopped her in her tracks:

"I can't wait to see who you become."

Grey could tell he'd been wondering whether or not to say that out loud. She felt his words fill the space between them with compassion . . . maybe even love. Grey just couldn't figure out what Bob's words meant. She hadn't been able to think about much else since.

When did Bob become the philosopher? Did Grey have him pegged all wrong? Was she missing something really big? "Becoming" implied growth, or even change. Did he want her to become someone else? She couldn't figure out how Bob knew anything about her when he had only ever cared about leaving the barn.

The whole conversation reinforced both what Grey did and didn't know. She knew she wasn't meant to live in the woods. That was easy to figure out. But she didn't think she was meant to live in the barn, either. Like Bob's parting words, she seemed to fall somewhere in between the barn and the woods. Maybe she fell somewhere else entirely. Grey knew she wanted to live somewhere warm and safe. She knew she wanted to be important in that place. Grey just couldn't figure out where that place was, or why she wanted to be there.

Grey found somewhere to go at night where she didn't overthink things. She could just be herself. Miss Jay called these nights their "unplugged sessions."

On these nights, a few friends sat around the pond outside. The crickets always came in hot with a cool violin sound. The frogs brought a strong bass, and Grey belted out lyrics. The animals made up the music as they went. On some nights, the stars shot across the sky. The animals would pretend it was the crowd cheering for their sold-out concert, demanding an encore. Mock vanity built their venue on those balmy summer nights. These were the nights when they swore life couldn't get any sweeter. Miss Jay played her banjo. She provided both a beat and a sounding board for Grey's mounting questions about life.

Chapter Thirteen
The Phoenix Club

Grey woke up with new energy. She was very excited. It was the first Saturday of the month. On this very special day, the Jam Barn was transformed into the Phoenix Club. The Phoenix Club was built to shine a spotlight on the farm's freshest talent. The animals would perform tonight on the pop-up stage.

Grey watched everyone set up for the Phoenix Club. When the weekend guests finished picking berries for the afternoon, the farm dogs loaded the empty orchard buckets onto wheelbarrows and dragged them to the barn. The frogs formed rows to make sure everyone would have a seat. The youngest frogs slid under the buckets and bounced them into place.

The hummingbirds hung up twinkly lights from pillar to pillar across the length of the barn. Grey climbed a ladder and directed the spotlights. The beavers built the platform for the stage. Only the beavers could be trusted with that important job.

The animals set up VIP tables at the front, and the lightning bugs nestled in empty jam jars. Flowers lay in bursts of color on the tables. The red snakes guarded the special section. They linked together and then linked to fence posts, forming a rope. No one dared to cross the snake-rope without permission.

These nights brought out the best of the best. The most talented and most stylish animals went to the Phoenix Club. Some spent the entire month in between shows planning their outfits. The "Best Dressed" list always made the next week's issue of *The Buzzy Bark.*

Two of the farm's trend-setting influencers were Estelle the Sassy Skunk and Becca the Rambunctious

Raccoon. They always made the "Best Dressed" list. Becca was hosting the Phoenix Club that evening. The two friends were known for their one-of-a-kind fashion statements. They never missed the mark.

Estelle was a VIP everywhere she went. Reporters asked her who she was wearing. "Max Will," she answered. "He's the best designer on the mountain," she said as she strutted down the red ore "carpet" outside of the Jam Barn. The reporters wrote down the name. They gushed over Estelle's sleek cape. They also adored the platform wedge shoes she wore on her feet. The reporters watched in awe as she walked effortlessly into the barn. This wasn't her first rodeo, so to speak.

Grey had met Estelle many times on her walks with Miss Jay. Miss Jay and Estelle were complete opposites, but they were still very good friends. They respected each other. They knew they were unique in their own ways.

Grey always felt overwhelmed around Estelle. She never knew what to say or do when she and Miss Jay visited the skunk. Grey never felt cool enough to be around her. She watched the cameras follow Estelle. The skunk looked close to perfect, and Grey was very intimidated.

"Miss Jay!" Estelle yelled from across the room. She walked toward them. "Look at you, with those bracelets.

Love the necklace, love it all. We're performing together later tonight, right?"

"Of course we are!" winked Miss Jay. "The cat's been working on her vocals all week. This will be a good experience for her. Thank you so much for helping us!" And with that, Miss Jay turned and informed Grey that she'd be singing in the show while Estelle played bongos and she, Miss Jay, played banjo.

It felt like a stone had dropped into the pit of Grey's stomach. "Um, I am not getting on that stage, Miss Jay," she squeaked, completely terrified. "I'm not ready to sing in front of anyone who isn't sitting at the pond," Grey said breathlessly. "And now I'm the only barn cat. I'm still adjusting to this life. I don't want everyone to laugh at me. Besides, I have nothing to say. Nothing that anyone wants to listen to, anyway."

"Just say what's in your heart," Miss Jay advised. She would not take no for an answer. "No one judges you when you're real. They relate. Quit trying to figure out what you think everyone wants to hear and start telling *your* story instead. I know those words are inside of you, somewhere."

Everyone sat down to watch the first few acts. Grey tried to find the perfect words, but it felt impossible. She couldn't concentrate on anything. She was in a total state of panic. Miss Jay, however, was having a ball. She watched with delight as Rita the Robin rapped her new song, "Holla Hooray." Licky the Frog—famous for his country twang—was then joined by the legendary Jane the Lizard on piano. These two always drew a standing ovation, as much for their stage presence as for their performance.

During intermission, Estelle checked in with Miss Jay and Grey. They were performing next.

"Grey is very nervous," Miss Jay whispered to Estelle. "Would you mind giving her a boost—or better yet, a kick in the butt? She has to learn how to put herself out there and be vulnerable."

Estelle sat next to Grey and quietly said, "I'm going to fill you in on a little secret . . . a motto I live by. You ready?"

Grey nodded her head yes, but she didn't know if she could concentrate on anything that Estelle had to say.

"Let go. I can promise you, if you don't get up there, you'll think back on this night one day and wish you had been on that stage. Afraid you'll make a mistake? Big deal. I've made a thousand mistakes. Earn those beautiful stripes and enjoy the ride. Sing, dance, and remember to laugh. A lot. Life's way more fun when you do."

With that, the lights dimmed, and Becca announced

the next act. Grey watched as Estelle turned and walked onto the stage.

Estelle was glorious. It was like the stage was made for her. She owned every spotlight. She waved to each corner of the barn, and the crowd cheered in greeting. She sat at her bongos, each thoughtfully lined in red ribbon to complement her cape. She tapped out a beat.

As Miss Jay flew onto the stage, she made an elegant loop around the room, spreading her wings. She reminded the crowd just how cool she was. Miss Jay smiled at Estelle as she landed. Taking her banjo, she found the rhythm with Estelle's beat and leaned into the groove.

Grey felt like she was going to throw up. She could hear her pulse beating in her ears.

Her mind raced. But it looked like Grey had no choice. She took a deep breath to steady herself.

Grey jumped onto the stage and grabbed the microphone. She could feel the spotlight on her, but she couldn't see a thing.

The words came as soon as she opened her mouth. Grey had no idea where they came from. She just stared straight ahead and heard the sound of her own voice:

"Scratch on my back, string me along,
I will perform and be beautiful.
Following suit to those before me,
My role seems undisputable.

"It's not always blue jays and bongos,
The barn life mundane of most days.
My voice is clear and my goals outspoken;
Follow, I'll show you the way.

"Saw the sun set while I
Searched the doorway for dreams.
Waiting for my moment to come;
There are lessons to learn, it seems.

"I long to spend the hours in vain,
Hearing the drumbeat of the pouring rain;
On a perch in a peaceful space,
Hoping I can rest without a trace."

14

Chapter Fourteen
Farm-Bred Foes

It was the kind of scream that could mean only one thing: destruction was sure to follow. The Widow knew that, once again, she'd have to run for her life. Make no mistake: there'd be grave consequences this time.

Suddenly, the Widow realized that she and the Hourglass had seen the plan in action. The ants were

NEVER late. The old desk NEVER slept in. This was the twitching hour the Hourglass had always talked about. This was the moment for which it would seek revenge. At first, everything moved in slow motion. Then, it all happened very fast. The ants didn't look up, not even once. They didn't scatter. They were small soldiers on a mission. Miss B followed their trail and jumped in fear when she saw the Widow. The Widow lunged for that tiny crack through which she'd entered the Jam Barn so many months ago. She wasn't as small as she'd been on that day, and she barely squeezed through. The Widow could hear the Hourglass laugh as she fumbled for safety. What a huge blow to the ego.

She ran away from the Jam Barn as fast as she had run to it. She'd been lured there by the sweet smell of jam. She left with the bitter taste of betrayal.

While the red light of the Hourglass grew dim to those it left behind, it would soon light the way for those on the other side. There were many animals on the farm in search of a leader, someone who could harvest their hate and feed into their fears. The Widow and the Hourglass were coming.

15

Chapter Fifteen
The Woodshed

The Widow quickly discovered that the Black Mountain Farm trails were a totally new world. She was in very different territory. The spring showers turned the mountain ore to mud, but her many legs pushed through the thick sludge. She hid from the lightning storms under fallen branches. Most animals would not have liked the rain, but the Widow enjoyed it. The sun dried out her skin.

The Widow considered their journey a means to an end. She thought it was as simple as finding a new place to live. The Hourglass, however, had a very different purpose in mind. Their journey meant much more to it. It would not falter or venture off the path, and it made sure the Widow remained focused. Their daily talks about life kept the Widow moving through her mounting fatigue. Each day, they woke with renewed determination for what the Hourglass assured her lay ahead: a new home.

She could feel the mountain watching as the Hourglass guided her to the Woodshed. It was once an important building on the farm. Now it stood empty because Mr. Joe had built new, fancier buildings near the main house. Isolated and forgotten, it made the perfect home for the pair. The Widow felt the Woodshed's sadness as soon as she saw it, but the Hourglass wouldn't let her back away.

"You can do this," it told her. "Don't think about that other place. They didn't want you there. They didn't appreciate you there. They didn't see your contribution or your strength. Be honest with the animals here. They'll have empathy for you. We can use that to our advantage."

The Widow entered through a worn crack in the front door, made some quick mental notes, and addressed the room.

"I'm the Black Widow of Black Mountain Farm. I was forced out of the barn. You were left behind. They feared me. They forgot you. I believe we can all benefit from my being here. I can provide you with a new purpose, but it's your choice."

Those who lived in Woodshed talked amongst themselves. They immediately agreed to welcome the Widow, happy to be involved in something again. The gloves clapped and the hedge clippers snapped. Even the old, warped tennis rackets from Mr. Joe's glory days strung together a tune. The Hourglass rewarded the room with a red glow. The Widow quietly wove her masterpiece of a new web by the wood stacks at the back of the Woodshed.

Mr. Joe only came to the Woodshed when he needed spare parts. The Widow and the Hourglass would be left alone here. They made themselves at home. The Hourglass came up with a plan to recruit a troop of animal workers. It sought insecurity above all. The more it sensed self-doubt, the more it shook with satisfaction.

The Widow used her charm to draw the animals in, but the Hourglass always sealed the deal.

The Widow slowly realized that the Hourglass was in charge of more than just the big decisions. The Hourglass controlled everything about her now. They moved to the Woodshed because of the Hourglass. They recruited workers because of the Hourglass.

The donkey in the nearby field was always alone. He was their first recruit. He would also be their most important.

16

Chapter Sixteen
The Pecking Order

Miss Jay knew that Grey was the talk of the farm following her performance at the Phoenix Club the night before. No one could get over the small cat with the big sound.

She watched as the cat seemed to float off the hay from a late afternoon nap. "I don't know if you know this, but I'm kind of a big deal," Grey joked. Well, she kind of joked. It felt good to feel important.

"Yeah, yeah. You had one night in the spotlight. Now listen to you!" she laughed. "It's probably time we had a talk, for your own good. I am sure you've heard things around the farm, and I want to make sure you know the facts. I think those facts should come from me."

Grey didn't like the sound of that, but she sat down anyway. "This doesn't sound like a good talk," she said warily.

"It's not bad at all," Miss Jay clarified. "It just is what it is. Things are old-school around here. Traditional. There's a pecking order, whether we like it or not. Take the bees, for example."

"We're not seriously talking about the birds and the bees, are we?" Grey asked, genuinely appalled. "That's not 'the talk' you're wanting to have, is it?"

"No, this is a different bee story," Miss Jay laughed. "See, the bees here have several jobs. First, they make honey. Miss B loves to use fresh honey in her kitchen, and many of the farm animals line up to "buy" what's left. The raccoons and skunks are always first in line, and they usually offer to trade something in exchange. Some years have paid better than others, but the bees had to brace for a few financial hardships because of the weather. Mrs. Pine saw the changes in weather coming, and she kindly offered the bees a key role in circulating *The Buzzy Bark* each week. The bees are a hardworking team; they had to step up to keep their hives afloat.

"The roosters and hens, too. The roosters are the first ones up every morning. They are responsible for waking everyone. Even Mr. Joe starts his day by their sound. The hens never complain, and they never leave their designated spots. They spend their whole lives producing eggs for the farm. It's not a glamorous job. They know that promotions are few and far between. But if you've ever peeked into the chicken coop late at night, you'll find that the chickens have more fun than anyone on the farm. Every night's a dance-off."

Grey had seen the bees deliver *The Buzzy Bark* each week. She sometimes stayed up late to watch the chickens practice their moves. They choreographed dances for the Phoenix Club. Still, Grey couldn't figure out where this conversation was going or why it mattered to her.

"Miss Jay, I appreciate your insight on the bees and the chickens," Grey noted, with just a touch of sarcasm. "What's next? The deer in the fields, or the fox in the woods?"

Miss Jay grinned. "Yes, let's talk about the deer. The deer graze in the fields. They are known for their strong, muscular bodies. You'll notice that the bucks have large antlers, which we call racks. The does are more delicate. We girls always talk about wanting doe-like features. Everyone loves to spot deer in the fields. However, the deer don't have it easy. Between the weekend guests and the coyotes, the deer constantly have to stay alert and look out for danger. Their beauty is actually a disadvantage in many ways. It makes them a moving target in the very fields they must visit for nourishment.

"The moral of the story is the same whether we're talking about the bees, the chickens, or the deer. We're all born into our roles. That's the way it's always been. You were born a barn cat. I know you want something bigger than that. I understand that you have goals and dreams. It's my tough job, however, to manage your expectations and make sure you know your role. We both know you're different: a star in your own right. For now, though, your stardom stays in the barn."

Miss Jay could see Grey absorbing the information even though she didn't like it.

"You know that I don't feel like a barn cat, right?" Grey asked. "I'm not saying I think I'm better than the barn. I'm saying I'm capable of so much more than just helping out with the mice. I can do that with my eyes closed. I'll die of boredom in the safety of the barn. Surely you see the irony." Grey stood up now, pacing back and forth. "Why can't I work hard and prove myself? You made me get on that stage to test my confidence. Well, it worked. Mission accomplished. I know in my gut that I'm destined for greater things. Don't you want to see me become an example of what's possible?" Grey tried hard to keep from shouting. She took a deep breath, but there was anger in her voice. "I need to take a walk and think about some things. Thanks for talking to me, Miss Jay." Grey turned and walked toward the chicken coops.

Miss Jay could tell that Grey was angry so she gave Grey some alone time for the night. She wanted Grey to be and do everything she set her mind to. As Grey's guardian, however, Miss Jay also felt a responsibility to tell Grey that life doesn't always work out the way we want it to. She didn't know what was in store for the cat. Miss Jay didn't want Grey to wake up one day and face a rude awakening. She would do everything she could to protect Grey and her dreams.

Become an example of what's possible.

17

Chapter Seventeen
Different Talk

Grey sat down near the chicken coops. She envied the chickens. They seemed content with this ridiculous pecking order Miss Jay told her about. The chickens still danced every night. What did they have to dance about? Their role in life wasn't glamorous at all. Grey couldn't imagine dancing right now. Her small corner on the bottom floor of the Jam

Barn already felt claustrophobic, and she hadn't even been there very long!

The system *had* to be broken if animals couldn't change and grow. What's orderly about a broken ladder? She was happy to claw her way up if that's what it took. Miss Jay would probably laugh if she knew that Grey stayed up most nights thinking of lounging on a plush blanket at the top. Sometimes she even pictured herself stretching out on a sofa inside a nice, warm house like the one Miss B and Mr. Joe lived in. Grey could almost feel the belly rubs.

She didn't dare talk about those dreams. Different day, different talk.

Chapter Eighteen

Donkey's Day Job

Jack the Donkey couldn't believe his luck. He felt like he'd won the lottery. He'd just gone out to watch the chickens. When he heard the whispers from the barn, he couldn't resist eavesdropping. This was amazing!

Jack was nothing special. He was a middle-aged donkey with graying fur and an extra bulge in his belly.

He had short legs, so it was hard for him to keep up with the other big animals. He also had big ears and a long nose, which embarrassed him. He'd always been insecure. Jack tried to distract others from his looks with loudness and jokes, but it didn't always work. The other animals on the farm often lost patience with him because he was always goofing off. He was sometimes accused of being stubborn, but Jack didn't think this was fair. Come to think of it, he very rarely thought anything was ever his fault at all.

The Black Widow discovered Jack a few days after she moved into the Woodshed. The building sat right next to the field where he spent most of his days. The Widow and the Hourglass found him sitting alone by the pond, feeling sorry for himself. They jumped at the chance to recruit him. They lured him to the Woodshed with promises of an easier, happier life.

The Woodshed didn't look like much on the outside. After all, it was just a place to store firewood. But the Widow and the Hourglass had transformed the inside. Jack quickly learned that the Woodshed's residents were also on Team Widow. Everyone in the Woodshed had a job to do. The gloves greeted Jack as he walked through the front door. They shook his hoof and showed him to the back.

Since no one really used the Woodshed anymore, it was the perfect hideaway. The Widow's web stretched along the entire back wall. The design seemed random, but they had a reason for everything. The Widow sat directly behind the wood stacks. She loved the dark shadows there. She and the Hourglass could spread out in the darkness and masterfully plan their next moves. Mr. Joe stored a few chairs and a rundown table in this part of the Woodshed, so it really felt like a little home to the Widow. After all, a home was all she really wanted.

Jack remembered every detail of that fateful day. The chairs motioned for him to sit. The Widow and the Hourglass spent hours putting Jack down. Then, they emphasized the exact ways in which only they could make him feel better. The Widow and the Hourglass told Jack that even though his ears were big, they were useful. He could listen in on nearby conversations. Though his legs were short, they kept him nimble and low to the ground. He wasn't a threat to those around him. His big nose could sniff out change, and he could bring back any news about what happened on the farm.

"You'll work for us," the Widow explained. "Keep an eye on the other animals and tell us where they are. We will make sure that you have everything you need. Your ordinary looks and everyone's low expectations of you will actually be a good thing for once."

Jack thought that if he played his cards right and if the Widow and the Hourglass told the truth, he could live a good life. He liked the idea of not having to be a working donkey anymore. Their plan seemed like a win-win solution in the beginning. Then he started working for them.

The Widow and the Hourglass made every decision for Jack: what he could eat, where he could go, when he had to come back. Jack lost any real friends he once had because he couldn't let anyone find out who he was working for. He'd gone from feeling insecure to isolated. Worse still, there was no way out. He had signed his soul away. He had to live each day doing what the Widow and the Hourglass wanted.

There'd been just one thing that Jack couldn't figure out. He had to admit that it made him a little nervous. Jack didn't understand why news from BMF mattered so much to the Widow or the Hourglass. They lived with the tools, far from all the animals on the farm, and they had the space to themselves.

"Why do you want to know what the others are up to?" he cautiously asked one day.

"We live here so no one will bother us," the Widow replied. "We want to keep it that way. We want to watch for any change or disturbance on the farm. We want to rule from a distance . . . at least for now. You keep us informed about the farm, and we will reward you accordingly. You will live a good life, as long as we all understand who makes the decisions around here."

Jack fell for it, hook, line, and sinker. He had no idea he was signing a life sentence or that he'd be one of many animals to fall under their spell. The Widow and the Hourglass used animals like puppets on strings. From the moment Jack signed on, he lost control over everything.

Since he felt like he had no other choice, he really did feel guilty sharing the young cat's story. But this was his new role in life.

"Her name is Grey, and Miss Jay never leaves her side. I can't figure it out, but it's clear that Miss Jay thinks there's something special about this cat. Don't get me wrong: Grey is beautiful, and she has really fast reflexes. I've seen her move with lighting speed around that barn.

"Anyway, I overheard a long conversation between Grey and Miss Jay. The cat all but cried because she feels so strongly that she's meant to be more than a barn cat. Miss Jay tried to console her. She kept reminding Grey that there's a pecking order on the farm. An old-school system. The weird thing is, Miss Jay has been kind of contradicting herself with this one, and that almost never happens. It's like she's grooming Grey to be more than a barn cat, all while making sure the cat knows her place. Maybe it's a lesson in gratitude or values. Maybe Miss Jay has some new trick up her sleeve. It's unusual."

The Hourglass lit up the entire room. It felt like some shady parlor under a red spotlight. Jack hated the red light. It always freaked him out.

"Well done, Jack," the Widow whispered with a smile.

Jack found it odd that the Widow seemed to be collecting herself, but what did he know? "Tomorrow, find a way to bring Grey to the Woodshed," the Widow continued, louder this time. "It must be tomorrow, and Miss Jay cannot know. We'll make sure you are rewarded handsomely for your extra effort."

With the plan firmly in place, Jack left the Woodshed. He tried to ignore the pit in his stomach. He kept telling himself that he had no other choice. He had to tell the Widow about Grey. She would have found out one way or another, so it might as well have been through him.

At least this way he'd be rewarded for his good work. He just hated that this was his job. Looking back on it now, there were so many things he'd do differently. "Wouldn't it be something if you could determine your own worth?" he mused aloud to himself. He thought about how different the view appeared in the rearview mirror at this later stage of his life. Ugh. "What's done is done," he sighed. When the Widow had her eye on someone, very little could be done to protect them.

Now Jack just had to figure out how to make his big move and be cool about it at the same time. Being cool wasn't exactly his strong suit.

19

Chapter Nineteen
Game Day

The Widow had been sitting in the shadows of the firewood, so Jack didn't see her initial reaction to the news about Grey. The donkey didn't realize the Widow's body had begun to tremble until the Hourglass lit up the entire room. They knew this cat was different. So did Miss Jay. They could all sense it. This was the opportunity the Hourglass had been waiting for.

"Let the games begin," it hissed.

20

Chapter Twenty
Fly By

Miss Jay didn't sleep well. She woke very early that morning after tossing and turning all night. She couldn't fight the feeling that something was . . . off. Miss Jay knew her conversation last night with Grey had been heavy, but that wasn't making her feel this way. She couldn't place her nerves, and that was highly unusual for her. It was time for a fly by. The cat was still sleeping soundly as Miss Jay wrote a quick note: "Gone for a quick trip around the farm to clear my head. Stay put, and don't get into any trouble! I'll be back by lunch. X, MJ"

21

Chapter Twenty-One
A Sketchy Reward

Grey rolled over on her blanket, blinking away sleep. She saw Miss Jay's note. Grey was glad to have the morning to herself. She needed more time to process last night's conversation. Grey loved Miss Jay, but she just couldn't shake the feeling that she was destined to be more than a barn cat.

She crawled off of her bed, stretched out her long

legs, and went for a walk. If Miss Jay had gone on one of her meditation flights, then Grey could certainly run to the pond and back to collect her own thoughts. She'd just rounded the corner of the barn when she walked straight into Jack's short legs.

"Oh, hi Jack! I'm so sorry. I'm clearly in my own world. I wasn't paying a bit of attention," she rambled in the form of an apology.

"No worries at all. Are you on your way somewhere?"

"Yeah, I was just taking a quick walk to the pond and back."

"Mind if I join you? I was planning to go to the pond later today. I'd prefer to go with you, if you're up for it."

Grey was surprised to hear the donkey speak, let alone ask to join her. Jack never interacted with the other animals. He was a total loner, and kind of weird. He was always around, but he was never really engaged. She couldn't tell if he genuinely didn't want friends or if he was just afraid of close relationships. Grey felt a little sorry for him.

"Sure, you can join, Grey replied. "What's new with you?" Grey could tell she'd caught Jack a little off guard. He appeared to be looking for the right words.

I have a friend who's going through a tough time, and I'm trying to figure out how to help her," Jack began.

"She's a bit different, so she keeps to herself. She can be intimidating, so she's had a hard time making friends on the farm. They misjudge her, and they assume she thinks she's better than everyone else. That's not true at all. She's actually got a lot to say, but she's kind of shy. She retreated to the Woodshed to get away from the farm gossip. I've known her for a while, but I've never seen her quite this sad. I'm trying to show her that it's okay that she's different from everyone else here. Let me know if you have any ideas."

Jack's words stunned Grey. It was like he had read her mind. He had described exactly how she felt. *She* had a hard time making friends. *She* knew that the other animals talked about her behind her back and said things that weren't true. She'd been going through this exact same thing for months. Grey wasn't sure that she could help Jack's friend find a solution, but they could talk about their similar experiences. Grey wanted to meet this mystery friend.

"I don't have any idea how to fix it, but I do understand how she feels," Grey offered. "I'd love to meet your friend some day and let her know that she's not alone."

"Oh, wow," Jack replied quickly. "That'd be wonderful. I can totally take you to see her now, if you're free. I know she's alone, and I'm happy to make the introduction. From there, you can stay in touch as often as you want."

Grey thought about it. She couldn't think of another opportunity to meet Jack's mystery friend. She knew Miss Jay would demand more information. She might not even let Grey go. Grey thought of what she would say to Miss Jay when she came back to the barn. After all, Miss Jay did say Grey was supposed to put herself out there.

"Lead the way," Grey confirmed.

They walked toward the Woodshed, talking about everything and nothing. They talked about the spring weather and *The Buzzy Bark.* The donkey was pretty funny. He could also be very thoughtful. Grey could tell he was creative. She wondered what he liked to do.

"Jack, it doesn't seem that you take life too seriously. What interests you?" She hoped the question didn't offend him.

Grey could tell by Jack's sideways glance that he was taken aback. She followed by quickly adding, "I don't mean to pry. I understand if the question is too personal. I just don't know much about you."

"Back in the day, I'd grab a stick and find any place to sketch," Jack finally replied. "I loved to capture the scene in front of me. It's always interested me that each of us could see the same thing from a completely different viewpoint." The donkey smiled. "Wow. I haven't thought of that in years."

As he talked, Grey saw the Woodshed ahead. She was excited to meet who she hoped would become a new friend. She followed Jack inside, and gasped.

22

Chapter Twenty-Two
The Silent Scream

The inside of the Woodshed was set up in two parts. Grey walked in and saw the hoes, hedge clippers, and gloves hanging on the shelves. All of the gardening tools were neatly arranged. This small section up front was not the main room, though.

Grey felt a lump in her throat, but she couldn't scream. She couldn't even speak. The sound wouldn't come out. Her agile legs and quick feet felt glued to the ground. She saw the wood stacks first, all lined up in rows along the back wall. The stacks cast dark shadows in every direction. Two chairs and a table sat in front of the wood, but she thought it odd that Mr. Joe came here to sit around.

Grey saw light glistening on a huge web that covered the entire back wall. It was a work of art. A Black Widow sat very still in the middle of the web. It was like the Widow was presenting herself in all of her eerie glory. Grey wondered if she was expected to become the Widow's next fawning audience and applaud.

Grey noticed that, though the Widow was small, her presence was overwhelming. The Widow's legs danced along her web, daring someone to watch them. Her eyes penetrated Grey. As the Widow slowly made her way down to eye level, Grey saw the red Hourglass on her back. It was connected to the Widow's spine, yet it seemed to have a mind of its own. Oddly, it looked like it steered the Widow. The Hourglass whistled as the Widow walked, setting her pace. They looked Grey up and down, sizing up the situation as much as the cat.

Grey carefully approached the web and met the pair face to face. The Widow smiled a smile that wasn't a smile at all. She motioned for Grey to take a seat. As Grey slowly sat, she realized that Jack had stayed at the front of the room, watching with his back against the wall.

Chapter Twenty-Three

The Worker's Decree

The Widow was eager to get through the formalities.

"It is so nice to officially meet you," she said through her fake smile. "I must say, I have heard a lot about you, Grey."

"I wish the same were true for me. I realize now that the donkey lied to get me here."

"Well, then, let me explain the situation and how I think we might be of service to you.

"We know you're not a typical barn cat. You're too smart for that. Forget your good looks: you can out-think the other animals. This makes you a poor fit for the role. You'll get bored, if you're not already. That doesn't benefit anyone.

"We think we know a way for everyone to gain from your skills. We are prepared to offer you a rewarding deal. It's called the Worker's Decree. It's a document that we all sign. I'll walk you through the details, and the Hourglass will prepare the terms as well as the timeline for you to reach your decision.

"Simply put, you'll want for nothing. If you want a family, we've got you covered. We can introduce you to a wonderful cat named Tom. Not interested? Not a problem. We'll get you what you want. You can still sing at the Phoenix Club. *The Buzzy Bark* will cover what you wear to the event. You will become an over-night sensation with more influence over the farm than you could possibly imagine."

While the Widow spoke, "Hermeow" bags appeared in the web out of nowhere. They overflowed with cat treats. The smell of the treats almost knocked Grey out of her chair. The Hourglass presented a laser light show along the shed walls. Grey watched a rainbow of colors float through the room. The Hourglass then spotlighted squeaky mice dangling from the rafters above. Next came the "string quartet." The old tennis rackets strummed as dust balls bounced between them. Grey was swept up. Her head followed the balls from side to side as if she were in a trance.

As Grey reached for a tempting treat, the light disappeared. Darkness fell over the room. A chill came over the cat as she regained her wits. She noticed that the Hourglass was ticking loudly.

"Can you be a little clearer about what you want from me?" Grey asked. "What's the price to want for nothing?"

"I'm glad you asked," the Widow continued. "Here's the deal. You get a life without worry. Anything you want will be available to you. You'll gain access to every pleasure the farm has to offer, and you'll be the star of the show every day.

"In exchange, you'll work for us. You see, Jack can only go so far. He can eavesdrop on conversations, as he did with you and that blue jay. But he'll never carry the kind of weight that you will. You'll be our eyes and ears in every situation, with special access to Miss B and the Jam Barn. It's a very common arrangement, one based on forgoing control over your future so that you can enjoy the fruits of life. That's the price you pay."

"But what if I don't want you making all the decisions?" Grey pushed back. "I never said I wanted someone else to choose my path for me." Grey was offended by the very nature of the Worker's Decree.

"That's up to you to decide, but, yes, let me be clear. You have two choices before you, and they are non-negotiable. You may choose to sign the decree, and we'll give you everything you want, as promised. Or, you can decline the offer. If you decline, you will be forced to leave the farm immediately." Grey's eyes went wide. The Hourglass beamed. "Let me rephrase. You will *want* to leave the farm immediately. We have unlimited resources. You don't want to be on the wrong side of this. You don't want to go into battle with us."

Grey swallowed hard, but her mouth was dry. "How long do I have to make my decision?" she asked quietly.

"Great question. The Hourglass will guide us. Hourglass, please share the terms and the timeline."

The Hourglass stopped ticking and whispered something to the Widow.

"You have two days to decide," the Widow said. "If you agree, we expect you to return to the Woodshed by the end of the second day. You must come alone. Otherwise, we will assume you have chosen a different path, and you better hope we don't cross it."

Grey took a deep breath and begged her body to move. She felt limp and heavy. She acknowledged that she understood the Worker's Decree, and she stepped away from the table. Grey paused to make sure that the Hourglass wasn't going to strike her, and then she walked toward Jack and the front door. Jack wouldn't make eye contact. Grey reached the doorway and didn't look back.

Grey ran as fast as she could. She wondered how the donkey would have captured this scene in his sketches. She hoped it flashed through his dreams and haunted him at night. She didn't stop running until she reached the Jam Barn. She kept telling herself that Miss Jay could fix this. Miss Jay could fix everything. She always did.

24

Chapter Twenty-Four
When the Fixer Fails

Miss Jay was in a frenzy. "Where have you been? Why are you running? What's wrong?" she asked question after question as Grey ran up to the door of the Jam Barn.

"Miss Jay, I'm so sorry," Grey gasped. "I've made a terrible mistake. Jack the Donkey tricked me into meeting the Black Widow at the Woodshed, and she presented me this thing called the Worker's Decree. If I sign the decree, I'll go work for the Widow and the Hourglass. They want me to share the inside scoop on the Jam Barn and manipulate all the other animals on the farm." Grey paused to catch her breath. The whole situation made her very sad. "I had the best intentions today. I thought I was going to make a new friend. I thought she would be like me," Grey sniffed. "The Hourglass said I only have two days to decide if I'll sign the Worker's Decree. If I don't sign it, I'll be forced to leave the farm for good."

"Let's back up to the part about intentions," said the steady bird, her head feathers standing straight up. "What is the Black Widow's intention here? It's not about having control over YOU. It's about having control over *everyone*: a firm foothold on the whole farm. I wonder if she thought of this plan before you even arrived at Black Mountain Farm."

Miss Jay wasn't ready to share the magnitude of that potential realization yet, or the source of her real worry. Instead, Miss Jay opened her wings. Grey fell against her bright white chest and cried and cried and cried. Miss Jay knew Grey wanted more than to live on the bottom floor of the Jam Barn. Much more. Miss Jay really believed Grey could be successful on her own. However, that was Grey's decision to make.

Grey sat up, sniffling, and wiped her eyes with her paws. She asked the one question that Miss Jay couldn't answer. "What do I do?" she quivered.

"This isn't a decision I can make for you," Miss Jay sighed. "You have to listen to your heart on this one. Oh, dear Grey," she murmured, drawing the cat in for another hug. "Wait a minute . . . oh, DEER! Yes, a DEER! I think I know who can help you. We absolutely must go see Biggie the Deer!"

"Biggie?" asked a bewildered Grey. She pulled out of their hug. "I'm sorry Miss Jay, but you're not making sense anymore. How can some random deer in the woods help me at all?"

"Biggie is a legend," Miss Jay declared, already collecting her things. "He never meets a stranger. What you see is what you get. He's lived on the farm his whole life. No one knows the land like Biggie. He'll guide you."

Miss Jay took off, giving a shaken Grey no choice but to follow her. The two set off to find the solution to Grey's problem through an old, dear friend. Miss Jay knew just where to look.

25

Chapter Twenty-Five
Big Softie

Biggie knew he was a large deer. Everyone always said he was "a strapping, strong buck." He was an old soul who preferred the simple pleasures in life and had no time for tricks. He didn't care for showy animals who talked about how much they had or how they got it.

Biggie towered over the other animals. He was front

and center wherever he went. He'd learned to use his size to his advantage. Biggie never met a stranger. He was very funny. He had perfected the art of self-deprecating jokes. Biggie's strength and humor made him very popular. Everyone felt drawn to him.

Biggie was comfortable entertaining crowds. He could perform on command. But that's what it was: a performance. Biggie knew the importance of a small group of good friends. These friends would still be there for him when he wasn't "being Biggie." It took some animals a long time to understand the difference between the performing deer and the private one. The private one became more prevalent following the accident.

Biggie thought back to that beautiful, yet fateful spring day. He remembered the doe's smile like it was yesterday. They were on Renee Way, a peaceful trail facing the east side of the mountain. She'd watch him, and then he'd watch her: what a dance. Biggie loved to flirt. He had to get her name. Biggie was so captivated that he didn't realize they had company. He didn't hear the coyote sneak up on them. A twig snapped and brought Biggie back to his senses. He and the doe locked eyes. They acknowledged the moment with small smiles before running for safety in separate directions.

To protect the doe and draw attention to himself, Biggie jumped higher than normal. On any other day, the jump would have been considered a clear mistake. Biggie knew that a trained eye would spot him. He was right. The coyote chased after him, but Biggie knew the mountain better. He side-stepped a low fence on the trail, but not before getting tangled up. He felt a tear. The left side of Biggie's head felt lighter as he pushed through. He instantly knew that his struggle left a mark. He just didn't know how deep a mark. Biggie certainly wouldn't have guessed that it might actually provide an opportunity for his real power to take the place of his missing antler.

Biggie's rack would never be the same after that day. He'd never be the showman he once was. He lost some friends after his accident, but they weren't his friends for the right reasons, anyway. The ones who stood by him were real, and they emerged with an unbreakable bond of loyalty. He'd been humbled, and he survived. It definitely took some time to see his incident that way. His thick coat grew whiter with each passing season, but the mischievous twinkle in his eyes stayed the same.

Chapter Twenty-Six

Station II

Biggie had watched Station II for a while. He knew it was moving day when he heard cranking sounds and the unmistakable deep hum of tractors. Station II was a small barn built to store fishing rods and tractors, but it wasn't really strong enough to withstand the elements. When Mr. Joe realized this, he moved all of his favorite possessions to a newer, shinier barn closer to his house. Biggie saw the opportunity to move in. His buddy, Cue the Rabbit, helped him out. Cue had been by Biggie's side since they were young: a big deer and a little rabbit. They were a heck of a pair. Cue was always the first friend to show up, in good times and in bad. Biggie often joked that that made Cue a rare hare.

Biggie had waited and hoped for this day because Station II was the perfect spot for his peaceful recovery. Biggie hadn't just sustained a physical injury in his accident. He had experienced a mental reset. He knew he was in a rut when he kept asking himself, "If I can't be what everyone wanted, then who am I?" Biggie was still big. Still funny. Still fast. But his antlers wouldn't look the same ever again. Deep down, he knew his antlers didn't define him, but he needed time to figure it all out.

It had taken months to decorate Station II. Biggie was really proud of the final product. He made the light fixtures out of old moonshine bottles. The room glowed warmly. He'd found mismatched chairs and furniture all over the mountain. Miss B had discarded most of the pieces, so the patterns were pretty hysterical. Heavy on the floral.

Biggie hung an old neon Gulf sign over the bar. He thought it made a good metaphor for the two types of animals on the farm. Some animals do what they say they're going to do, and some animals don't. The gulf between the two grew wider every day. The neon sign was almost as important to the bar as Miss B's "'shine." It sat on the top shelf. Biggie had seen many moons with that special sauce. Music often played in the background. Biggie was told he was quite the dancer.

Biggie kept every copy of *The Buzzy Bark*. He liked supporting BMF, Mr. and Mrs. Pine, and the bees. Nothing made him happier than seeing his friends in the paper's "Hometown Honey" profile. He hung up those profiles next to the signed bucks. That was one of Cue's brilliant ideas. Every Station II guest signed a "buck" when they came over. Guests left their autographs and messages on fake dollar bills to commemorate their visits. The bucks reminded Biggie of great nights with his friends. *The Buzzy Bark* profiles and signed bucks covered every wall.

Biggie loved the inside of Station II, but the outside was his favorite. He loved watching the sunset from the old front porch. That's where the trail sign décor came in. Mr. Joe couldn't figure out where his trail markers kept disappearing to. The "Buck Crossing" sign was a total treasure. Sometimes Biggie would grab a cold drink, sit on the bench, and cross his front legs, waiting for someone to catch the joke. He'd also found a metal rooster. He placed it in front of the screen door to greet guests. How he loved yard art.

Biggie knew that his style was eclectic. That might have been a vast understatement, but he loved Station II almost as much as he loved the deer he'd become over the years. Biggie wasn't sure that any of these treasures had made him bigger. However, they definitely made him stronger.

27

Chapter Twenty-Seven
Blackjack

Miss Jay and Grey made it to Station II after what felt like forever. Grey could hardly stand still because she was so anxious. "Now, wait here, Grey," Miss Jay instructed the squirming cat as they walked onto the porch. "Settle down, and I'll be out with Biggie in a moment."

Miss Jay laughed as she flew inside, always amused

by the ever-changing décor. The "new" sofa they'd swiped had an especially bold pattern.

"Well, guys, I suppose you've heard," she inquired, more as a greeting than a question. "It seems the Black Widow left the Jam Barn to set up shop in Mr. Joe's Woodshed. She and the Hourglass recruited Jack the Donkey to spy on animals all over the mountain. Jack was easy bait. He's apparently eavesdropped on conversations for quite some time. I don't know how many other animals the Widow and the Hourglass have forged alliances with, but I think we can all agree that we've solved the mystery of the quiet coyotes."

She paused to let the news settle in. Biggie and Cue didn't budge, so she kept going.

"Jack lured Grey to the Woodshed. He promised Grey she would make a new friend. She would meet someone who would understand her. He played to every one of Grey's insecurities.

"Of course, Grey had never heard of the Black Widow. We don't discuss her in the Jam Barn. This may sound crazy, but I think that the Widow and the Hourglass are staging a takeover of Black Mountain Farm.

"From the sounds of it, they gave Grey one spectacular show, too. They had bags filled with cat treats, and the Hourglass tossed in a laser light show. Can you imagine? Then the Widow dropped what they're calling 'the Worker's Decree' on a dusty old table, and the Hourglass gave Grey a deadline. She only has two days to decide her whole life. Become a spy, or become Grey. On or off the mountain. Just like that." Miss Jay stomped on the floor for effect.

"It's not surprising," offered Cue. "I mean, Grey's a beautiful cat. Everyone watches her. She's purrfect," he joked. The other animals gave half-hearted laughs at his attempt at humor. "In all seriousness, if the Widow is building a team, I'm sure she sees Grey's potential. Miss B immediately liked Grey. An alliance with the cat would give the Widow and the Hourglass access to the family *and* the Jam Barn. It's like hitting twenty-one every time. Blackjack, poker, call it what you want. They're playing a game. That game will affect Grey's future. She should have as much information as possible if she's going to make this important decision."

"We also know that this is bigger than Grey," Miss Jay chimed in. "Mr. and Mrs. Pine chose me to be Grey's guardian when she was born. They didn't say why."

Biggie sat quietly for what seemed like days. It was actually these thoughtful moments, as he sat with a furrowed brow, that his closest friends loved most about him. He carefully pulled out his old pocket watch, a treasure he'd found in his youth. As though reading the broken dial for a decision only he could see, Biggie spoke directly to Cue.

"Help me pack up. It's time to go see Bo on the mountain."

Miss Jay watched as Cue nodded. She heard him sigh deeply.

"You know it's never an easy journey to reach Bo," Cue replied, a slight whine in his voice. He paused and appeared thoughtful. "Then again, it shouldn't be."

To lighten the mood, Cue turned toward Miss Jay and winked. "Don't let Biggie eat too many berries on the way up," he instructed. "He's trying to shake off a few pounds, for the ladies."

Biggie laughed as he gathered his things. And his courage.

Chapter Twenty-Eight

Whipped In

Bo the Wise Owl felt like a parent to the animals who passed through his part of the mountain. He knew he played a major part in their lives. He took the part very seriously. Even though parents weren't supposed to choose favorites, Bo had to be honest: Biggie was certainly his favorite. Bo looked after Biggie like a father would.

Bo and Biggie were very similar. It was easy to see why they got along so well. They both had magnetic personalities. They were both leaders. Bo admired the giant deer's gentle heart. He loved that Biggie was never afraid to make everyone laugh, especially when it would cheer up others.

Bo smiled at the memories. It took months to reach the moment when Biggie came back to himself after the accident. His big wit, so much larger than his big body, returned. Bo was worried that Biggie had lost himself in the accident. Bo spent weeks begging Biggie to tell him about the beautiful doe. He wanted Biggie to describe the scene as though there'd been no accident at all.

Biggie finally caved with the help of a little liquid courage. He stood to reenact the moment, always the perfect storyteller.

"So, I made my way down the mountain. Slid into position on the far field. I threw up my front leg—and my will—to feel the air. It was still and crisp, like a fresh dollar bill. I lowered my hoof and hung steady. Smooth. Like a stallion. I was ready. I whipped in for a fresh piece of grass . . ."

And just like that, with a dramatic leap that began somewhere around the phrase "whipped in," Biggie lost his footing and slid across the floor. He could have braced himself, but he refused to let go of his drink. Head over tail, all three hundred pounds of him, Biggie landed.

He still held his cup firmly in his hoof. He turned toward Bo, cocked his head to the side, and placed the now-empty cup in his reshaped rack, the same rack whose reflection he'd hid from for months. The combination of his antlers and the empty cup formed a new trophy. It was the mark of resilience.

"That, Bo," Biggie chuckled, "is what you call nailing the landing, 'whipped in' cup and all." Biggie pretended to drop a fake microphone, not to be confused with the cup.

From that moment on, the "whipped in" story would result in a newly named 'Wipi cup' that Biggie sometimes carried on what remained of his left antler. The cup contained a fresh new outlook on life, ensuring his friends that all was not lost for the deer. Biggie's gift, after all, had always been his humor.

29

Chapter Twenty-Nine
Ride or Die Friends

Biggie stepped onto the porch and took a seat on the bench beside Grey. "So, you met the Black Widow. It seems we have a bit of a situation," Biggie mused to his new friend. "You can stay here on the farm. You will secretly work for the Widow and the Hourglass. To an outsider looking in, your life will look perfect. You'll be the envy of every animal. But that new life has a price. You'll report your every move and any news from the farm. You will do whatever the Widow and the Hourglass say. Simply put, they will own you."

While Biggie spoke, he watched Grey stand and pace back and forth on the porch. Grey clearly absorbed every word he said, but she also studied Station II. She looked at all of the trail signs and personalized décor that made this Biggie's home. He saw Grey smile at the signed bucks and the profiles from *The Buzzy Bark* as she peeped through the screen door.

"Could you do it, Biggie?" Grey finally asked. "Could you sell out to the Widow?"

"Or," Biggie offered, determined to keep Grey on track, "you can leave Black Mountain Farm behind and make a different life. One with the freedom to live out your own destiny. You'll learn what makes you happy. Who knows, you may also like signed bucks!" he said with a wink. "But when you leave, you'll take a big risk. Believe me when I tell you there are no guarantees in life."

Biggie watched as Grey turned to look him directly in the eye. She was ready to face this problem head on.

"So . . . what's the next step?" Grey asked, staring the situation down squarely. Miss Jay and Cue the Rabbit stepped outside as soon as Grey spoke. Biggie acknowledged them with a sweep of his hoof.

"We've all agreed that Miss Jay and I will take you to visit our friend Bo the Wise Owl, at the top of the mountain. Bo sees all. He functions at a different frequency than other animals. He doesn't judge any of the choices we make. His purview stretches not just miles, but millennia. He will help you find peace with your path."

Biggie stood and grabbed his Wipi cup from Cue. He then leaned over and whispered to Grey with a smile, "Hop on the rack, darlin'. She's not the grill she once was, but she can still get 'er done." Biggie stepped off the porch, laughing. He secured the cup to his broken antler. He nodded at Grey, insisting that getting into the cup on his head and traveling up the mountain was her next step.

Biggie watched as Grey assessed him and the Wipi cup on his head. He could see her thinking through the entire situation before her. He watched Grey's eyes flick from his back to his head. Biggie guessed that Grey was trying to figure out how to jump onto his back, climb up his neck, and carefully get around his deformed antler so she could crawl into Biggie's custom cup. That was her seat. This journey was her only chance for answers. He smiled as Grey took a deep breath and hopped on for the most important ride of her life.

30

Chapter Thirty
Send in the Clowns

Jack was on his way back to the Woodshed when he saw the red light. He'd gone on a walk to sort out the madness of the day. The Hourglass always flashed a red beam on the field when it was time for him to report for duty.

It had been like watching time in reverse. He saw his life flash before his eyes. He had been that cat. He had been in that chair. They had assured him that working for them was the answer to all of his problems. An easy out. As the Widow and the Hourglass spoke to Grey, Jack remembered the saying, "If it sounds too good to be true, it probably is." He couldn't even look at Grey as she walked past him on her way out of the Woodshed.

"What have you heard?" the Hourglass demanded as he walked into the Woodshed.

"Not much to report yet," Jack shared. "I snooped around the Jam Barn, but Grey wasn't there. I got as close as I could without being seen. I heard someone mention something about a deer, but who knows?"

They knew who. Or "hoo", rather, if their hunch was correct. Things just got interesting.

"We know where they're going," the Hourglass replied. "And we know their plan. Send in the clowns."

Jack cringed. He hated when the Hourglass called the other animal workers clowns. Sometimes it called them puppets. It just depended on the day. He didn't want to think of himself as a clown . . . but right now, he sure felt that way.

"Miss Jay is taking Grey to see her friend, Biggie," the Hourglass continued. "Biggie will guide them up the mountain. We'll send a few Team Widow success stories to meet them along the way. It might help Grey see just how much we can do for her."

"Sure thing, boss," Jack mumbled on his way out the door. Success stories. Right.

31

Chapter Thirty-One
Recipe for Disaster

Jeri the Fox knew the system before she even knew there *was* a system. It was in her blood. She was a natural shapeshifter. She told other animals what she thought they wanted to hear. Jeri had no problem making something up to gain extra confidence.

Jeri couldn't remember a time when she didn't pull out all the stops. She knew her strengths. She could blend in on any side of any deal. For example, when she needed something from the trees, she became their friend. She told them how sturdy and strong they were. She made each tree feel like it had the best and most important place on the mountain. She would earn the trees' trust and get what she needed from them. Then she would move on to the squirrels. Or the birds, or the beavers. She made friends with anyone in need. She positioned herself in the middle as a trusted "friend" to all. However, Jeri's friendship came with a price. Just a little something for the effort. She loved benefitting from the fruits of everyone else's labor.

Jeri had always been good at making deals. Now, thanks to the Widow, dealmaking was a piece of cake. The Widow was the only animal that Jeri had ever really considered an equal. For that reason, Jeri was cautiously optimistic when the Widow approached her. All Jeri had to do was keep the Widow in the loop. In turn, the Widow would have Jeri's back if any of the fox's deals went south. Jeri had made a few shady deals lately, so the Widow's support made Jeri feel safe.

Jeri thought back to her deal with the coyote. She really thought that she had met her end. Many seasons ago, she'd crossed the wrong path at the wrong time and found herself standing face to face with a serious foe. There'd been nowhere to run. That's when she remembered: the one thing the coyote wanted more than a fox was a strong, strapping buck. Jeri had just closed a deal with a young buck. Ironically, she told the buck she would guard the trails. She knew she could bait the coyote with the bigger animal.

"I have an idea," Jeri carefully pitched to the coyote. "I know where you can find something you want more than me. I know where you can find him right now." She broke her deal with the buck and told the coyote where he was as casually as if she were sharing a recipe. Jeri watched the coyote run off for the bigger, better meal.

That was the day Jeri decided to partner with the Widow. She called it Decree Day. The last thing Jeri needed was another coyote coming after her, and, as promised, the Widow took care of the issue. Jeri's peace of mind returned, and she didn't spend a second thinking about the consequences. As she always said: "Don't hate the player, hate the game."

32

Chapter Thirty-Two
Paintbrush Path

Biggie knew the mountain trails inside and out. He'd grown up here. He guarded them just as he guarded the guest he carried. He'd spent many seasons in these woods, and he knew of all her inhabitants. No animal could fool him. Very few tried anymore due to Biggie's experience and intuition.

Each mountain trail was unique. The Pine family

protected some of the trails. Other trails wrapped around sun-soaked ponds and lakes. The flowers and animals chose neighborhoods based on their preference for sun, water, or shade. Mr. Joe and Miss B had created many trail maps over the years. They tried to capture the twists and turns of the paths to guide the weekend guests to the best views.

Biggie and Miss Jay didn't need a map. The group took the first turn onto Paintbrush Path. Biggie pointed out: "This trail is known for its beauty in the spring. Some of the flowers you see are called Indian Paintbrush because it looks like the land was painted with bright strokes of orange." The Paintbrush loved recognition, and they greeted the group with a wave.

"The trees with the white buds are known as Dogwood. They only bloom for a few special weeks of the year. This trail is one of Miss B's favorites. She says it feels like her own secret garden."

The soft, white petals chattered above them. Biggie smiled. He'd missed their conversations. Even though Grey was new to the mountain, she could still appreciate this moment. There was always beauty in the cycle of changing seasons.

As they walked, Paintbrush Path turned into a moving canvas of colors. The red ore rose to meet the orange Paintbrush. The white Dogwood petals reached for the blue sky. The three travelers were distracted by the beauty around them. They didn't notice Jeri lurking behind the colorful brush.

"I caught wind that you were on the mountain. I had to see it for myself," Jeri said with a smirk. Her suspicious eyes fell on the small cat hunkered down in the cup on Biggie's left antler. "Well, well, well. What have we here?" she inquired, leaning forward for a closer look. Grey shrank back, squeezing as tight as she could into the Wipi cup.

Biggie knew that Jeri couldn't be trusted. She was a fast talker and a master manipulator. She always made promises that she had no intention of keeping. She was the very definition of a sly fox. She betrayed others when it helped her the most. He knew firsthand just how cunning she could be.

Chapter Thirty-Three

Along for the Ride

Grey peeked out of the Wipi cup and studied Jeri. She looked at Jeri's fur, she watched Jeri's body language, and she heard the tone of Jeri's voice. Grey felt something was off about the fox. She just couldn't figure out what.

Jeri was covered in thick, rusty-red fur that anyone would envy. She had brownish streaks down her shoulders and back which, at first glance, resembled a cross. The irony of this pattern was not lost on anyone who knew her. Her fluffy red tail ended with a white tip that matched her bright white chest.

"Jeri," Biggie said with a sigh. "We're just passing through," he said, and started to move around her.

Jeri wouldn't let the trio go that easily. She jumped in front of them and sat down, speaking directly to Grey.

"You know, I've been looking for a partner," Jeri smiled, exposing her sharp, white teeth. "I've been on the mountain for a long time. I have a reputation for making deals. It's all about who you know. I'm friends with important animals. I help negotiate arrangements between everyone here. Fish, birds, squirrels . . . you name it. I help them, and they help me."

Grey stayed silent, and Jeri kept talking. "Look at the squirrels. I find them the best trees to live in. In exchange, they share the fruits of their storage. I've struck deals with everyone and everything that you see up here. The older I get, the more I understand the value in partnerships. I'd love to work with someone like you. I bet we could reach some kind of arrangement."

Jeri paused, waiting for a reply. Grey watched Jeri's smile grow. The fox seemed confident that her words had captured the young cat's attention. Grey looked around.

Jeri was so laser focused on her target that she hadn't paid attention to the change in energy around them.

The flowers shook their heads at Grey, shouting, "NO!" The grasshoppers had lined up in a display of solidarity against Jeri. Grey saw it all, even though she didn't really understand why the flowers and grass-hoppers were acting this way. She also felt Biggie's shoulders sag. It seemed that just sitting in Jeri's presence made his back hurt.

"Thank you so much, Jeri, but I promised Biggie and Miss Jay that I'd just be along for the ride today. I'm sure our paths will cross again."

Biggie started walking away. Grey snuck a glance at the fox when they were farther down the path. She couldn't tell where Jeri's coat ended and the mountain's red dirt began. Given that she also couldn't tell where Jeri's sincerity started or stopped, the symbolism wasn't lost.

While she couldn't tell where Jeri's fur ended, Grey could clearly see the fox glaring back at her. She watched a snarl replace that fake smile. Grey would never forget the feeling in her gut when she realized that the fox was no good.

34

Chapter Thirty-Four
The Formidable Fox

Once they were out of hearing distance, Biggie told Grey about the day that everything changed for him.

"I first met Jeri when I was a young buck. At that time, I spent most of my evenings exploring the fields, playing around, and flirting. I was always on the lookout for coyotes and weekend guests. The guests just liked to look at me. The coyotes were the real problem.

"Jeri and I made a deal. She'd secure certain trails and make sure they'd be safe so I wouldn't have to keep track. One afternoon, she sold me out. She told a coyote where I was. I wasn't paying attention, and I barely survived. That was the day my antler broke.

"I retreated to a quieter, more private life. I eventually moved to Station II," he said. Biggie was quiet for a moment, thinking about all he'd been through. "Everything happens for a reason. Now I have the greatest cup holder on the mountain," he said with a wink.

Biggie hoped his story would help Grey understand just how careful she needed to be with animals like the fox. He had also hoped they wouldn't run into Jeri at all on their journey, certainly not right out of the gate.

Miss Jay, on the other hand, was more direct with Grey. "Jeri is two-faced. She says one thing and does another. She's known for this. She'll sell you on a deal with no plans of honoring it when the time comes. Jeri's also become a lot pushier. You have to be careful when you come across situations like that one back there. Remember: your instincts will guide you, if you let them."

Biggie had an instinct of his own. He sensed that Miss Jay had more to say and was keeping it to herself. Jeri hadn't appeared accidentally. Not on their first trail. He had a hunch Miss Jay thought the same thing.

Your instincts
will guide you,
if you let them.

35

Chapter Thirty-Five
Nervous Nelly

Nelly the Squirrel looked back on that fateful day almost every day. She had had the perfect house and the perfect kids. She built her nest from scratch. She built it before it had a "community" view. She built it because SHE had a view. A vision. She could see the lake, the Dogwoods, the Paintbrush, the birds: everything.

Her kids had hated the nest at first. It was too far away from all of their friends, so they never had visitors. Nelly became the playdate, the protector, and the provider, all wrapped into one champion of a mom. On pretty days, the family swam together in the lake, which, back then, was their private backyard. They competed to see who could swim a mile in the shortest time. Nelly made a patch to award each week's winner. Memories made patches, patches made quilts, and the quilts wrapped her kids in the kind of love only a mother could give.

Nelly watched in delight as new neighbors moved in. They trickled in slowly at the beginning. Everyone shared the space exactly as she'd imagined. Her kids were happy and made new friends. Word about the new space got out, which often happens when something's too good to be true. Nelly wasn't sure how so many animals discovered their quiet nook so quickly. The trees that once covered her family and guarded her privacy didn't help her anymore. That's when Jeri, the Widow, and the Hourglass came to visit.

Jeri explained that there would be new rules in the neighborhood because of all the new neighbors.

"You can always pay to play," the fox offered with a smirk. "Just know that you will pay a lot more in rent since so many animals want to live in this spot. Or . . ." the sly fox paused. She looked from Nelly to the Widow and back. "You can sign a different dotted line, and all your stress will disappear."

Nelly knew that at her age, it would be nearly impossible to work hard enough to pay higher rent. But she couldn't bear to make her kids move away to a new tree.

"Your house is the perfect watchtower," the Widow explained. "All we ask is that you keep track of who comes and who goes. This agreement is such a simple solution for everyone. You let us know if you see anything strange. In exchange, you get to keep your home. It will forever be filled with more nuts than your family can ever eat. Store or don't store. You won't spend another day worrying about food."

Nelly knew it would be very hard to stay in their home if she didn't take the deal. She had found this tree before anyone else. *Before the fox, or the frogs, or the beavers, or the ducks,* she thought. Nelly couldn't lose the only home her family had ever known. She couldn't see any solution other than the one sitting in front of her. She only saw the Widow, the Hourglass, and their Worker's Decree.

As Nelly signed the document, she knew she'd never see the view from her tree in the same way again.

36

Chapter Thirty-Six
Tree of Trust

After walking for what felt like hours, the trio finally stopped to rest awhile. Grey couldn't get enough of this place. There was something new everywhere she looked. The bass showcased their backstroke, swimming laps along the length of the lake. The beavers waved from their dams at the water's edge. Grey could spend days soaking up the sun and listening to the sounds of this lakeshore community.

"Welcome to Clear Lake Corner," Biggie said warmly. "It's a peaceful spot to rest before making the next steep hike. Miss B put these benches along the waterline," he swung his head toward some green and brown wooden benches near the water. "You can lounge here while I grab a quick drink. Enjoy yourself. This is a special hideaway."

Grey nodded in agreement. She stretched out on a bench to sunbathe. Grey took a minute to appreciate the community around her. Redbirds darted from tree to tree. They traded worms to make sure everyone's little ones had been fed for the day. The ducks quacked back and forth. They argued over whose turn it was to take a dip in the deep end.

Grey was just dozing off when a loud thud jolted her back to her surroundings. She looked up and saw a squirrel. She had just dropped a pile of nuts. "I'm so sorry!" the squirrel screeched. "I'm Nelly! Nice to meet you! These nuts just get heavier every year. But, if I'm being honest, my knees aren't as strong as they used to be, either." Nelly pointed to her wobbly knees with a nervous laugh.

Grey could see that Nelly was an older squirrel.

Nelly had honey-colored fur that was graying around her temples. Grey noticed that Nelly's colors matched her tree, reminding her of the many ways in which nature nurtured. Grey's mind flashed to an image of Jeri and her fur that matched the dirt. She hoped the sneaky fox hadn't received credit for that.

Nelly was very animated, and Grey could already tell she was quite the character. Nelly's wide eyes begged for attention.

Grey watched as Nelly picked up the dropped nuts and couldn't figure out why the squirrel seemed so frazzled. The setting couldn't have been more peaceful. Nelly carefully carried the nuts up to her nest. Hers was no ordinary nest, either. Grey could see from the bench that Nelly's home was overflowing with clutter. It probably needed a good spring cleaning.

"Is it okay if I come up?" Grey called to the scrambling squirrel. "I know you're busy. I've just never been in a squirrel's nest before. I'd love to join you!" Grey paused, sensing the squirrel's apprehension. "I promise you can trust me."

Nelly glanced at Biggie and Miss Jay for approval. They both nodded in agreement: Grey could climb up the tree for a quick visit. Grey slowly made her way up to the entrance of the squirrel's house and stopped as she poked her head in. She couldn't believe her eyes. There was so much . . . stuff. From the looks of things, Grey guessed Nelly was a bit of a hoarder.

Chapter Thirty-Seven

Room with a View

Grey stood in Nelly's entryway. A welcome sign hung just inside. Grey laughed at the "Nuts for You" doormat. There were boxes stacked on boxes of snakeskins, feathers, fishing wire, jelly worms, and picnic napkins. The sofa was covered with patchwork quilts that looked destined to become family heirlooms. Nuts lay scattered everywhere, in every nook and cranny.

Grey had expected more organization from a squirrel. She didn't mean to assume, but still.

"Don't judge the mess," Nelly begged nervously. "I never throw anything away. My mother raised me that way. You just never know, right?" she said with a nervous laugh. "Plus, the fast growth of the neighborhood resulted in new rules for everyone. That meant new arrangements for me. My new deal also provides plenty of nuts. As you can see, my storage system is overflowing with the extras. It makes my fur itch to think about the mess. However, there's plenty to eat, so I can't complain."

"Well, I'm happy that it all worked out for you, but these nuts don't have to make you nuts," Grey joked. "When was the last time you paused and looked outside?"

Grey moved over to the window with the beautiful waterfront view. The ducks dove off the dock. They splashed the frogs with their cannonball landings. It was priceless. Grey realized that Nelly could see the crossroads between Paintbrush Path and Clear Lake Corner from this window. Most animals would kill for this spot.

"Miss Jay always tells me to live in the moment," Grey said. She pointed to the lake. "Come watch! Otherwise, what's the point in having any of this?"

Even as Grey spoke, she could see that Nelly was somewhere else. Maybe she was still thinking about dropping the nuts. Maybe she was thinking of the past or worrying about the future. Nelly appeared to have lost touch with everything around her. She didn't seem to enjoy the view anymore at all. Grey guessed that all of her worrying made it hard for her to be happy.

Grey thanked Nelly for the visit. She slowly made her way down the tree. Biggie and Miss Jay had been listening from below. Grey climbed up onto Biggie's head and settled into the Wipi cup. She thought about the nervous squirrel. Grey promised herself that she'd always try to take in the view and appreciate the present moment.

Grey nodded off in the Wipi cup. She could hear Biggie's voice in the background. She was too sleepy to pay any attention.

"Arrangements, huh? This journey gets more complicated by the minute," Biggie murmured softly to Miss Jay.

Miss Jay nodded, silently acknowledging what neither of them wanted to say out loud.

38

Chapter Thirty-Eight
Hangover Hedge

Grey woke up from her nap. Her muscles ached. The Wipi cup was not a comfortable bed. As she stretched out her front legs, Grey gazed ahead at the final stretch of trail. She saw that Biggie was carefully maneuvering a narrow track along the mountain's edge. Miss Jay flew above them.

"This road keeps uninvited guests from reaching

the top," Biggie shared. He could feel Grey stretching. "It's a sharply curved trail. We all call it the Hangover Hedge. You can only climb it with a clear head. If you lack focus, it's a long and dangerous drop to the bottom."

Looking out at the horizon, Grey saw the daily routine of many animals. Cows grazed in the pastures, happy each day to find a fresh patch of dewy grass. Pigs splashed around in muddy troughs, giggling with delight. She could even see the goats as they escaped their pens, frustrating the local farmers.

Wisteria lined the edge of the trail. It sprayed Grey and Biggie with perfume as they passed. The air was sweet and the view was perfect. In the middle of such a beautiful day, Grey was shocked to see an animal lying deathly still in their path.

"Oh no!" Grey shrieked. "That animal isn't moving!"

39

Chapter Thirty-Nine
The Missing Missus

Biggie heard the panic in Grey's voice. He understood. The animal wasn't much bigger than the cat. If that weren't enough to freak Grey out, the creature was also stiff as a board. It had a ratlike tail and coarse, grayish-white fur. It also had a white face and a pink snout to match its pink fingers and toes.

Biggie stopped and stared at the frozen animal as

it lay on its side. He struggled to find the right words. Whatever he said now would have a bigger impact on Grey than their time on the trail. He paused, glancing in Miss Jay's direction. He then carefully explained the story behind the Missing Missus.

"That, Grey, is a possum," Biggie informed the confused cat. "She looks frozen because it's her defense mechanism. It's called 'playing possum.' She will lay there until no one else is around. Sometimes, she'll stay still for hours at a time because she doesn't feel comfortable talking to others. This is the only way she knows how to cope. We call her the Missing Missus because . . . well, because she forgot her own name." Grey gave a small gasp. She couldn't imagine what it would be like to forget who she was.

"The Missing Missus used to have it all. She was spunky, funny, and very talented. The Missing Missus had big dreams of becoming a star. She had the voice of an angel. She lit up the stage at the Phoenix Club. Even animals from other farms came to watch her perform. She knew possums weren't naturally in the spotlight, but she certainly had the pipes for it."

Grey listened intently. "I don't understand. If she had all of that going for her, what happened?"

"Well, it's not easy to follow your dreams. It's even

harder to watch them disappear. You have to believe in yourself, even when everyone else doesn't. Following your dreams takes a leap of faith. If you fail, you'll start over where you land. That's a hard lesson for anyone. The Missing Missus just started acting differently one day. We all assumed that she had either let her fear of failure or her critics overwhelm her."

Even as Biggie said that, he now knew the truth. The Missing Missus wasn't afraid to succeed. She'd had the personal resolve to fight the Widow's price for the good life. The Widow and the Hourglass had placed the Missing Missus in their path, so close to the end of their journey, to show Grey what happened when someone declined the Worker's Decree.

Biggie remembered how great the Missing Missus had been. She'd had that "it" quality about her. That one thing that no one could quite describe. It separated her from all the rest. The possum walked into a room and the air changed. Everyone knew she was going places. That's why her fall had been so hard to watch.

Biggie felt the same powerful energy from Grey. He'd be shocked if this cat wasn't going places.

40

Chapter Forty
What's That Sound

Biggie, Miss Jay, and Grey were long gone when the Missing Missus raised her head to acknowledge the fading sounds of their visit. She knew she'd heard voices. Maybe she even heard the faint sound of her own.

Chapter Forty-One

The Widow's War

What a motley crew. The donkey, the fox, and the old squirrel. The Widow sat above them, watching from her web. The clowns reported back with resounding success.

The Widow and the Hourglass had created a make-shift war room using the dusty table and chairs. The animals went around in a circle, recounting their stories one by one. The tools were standing by, ready to report for duty if and when needed.

"She was ALL IN," Jeri led. "Mesmerized. I even had the grasshoppers standing at attention. Grey could tell that I was the head dealmaker on the mountain. I'm sure Biggie has told her his story by now. The pieces just snapped into place. She knows that *we* decide who has a deal and who doesn't. We can give it, and we can take it away. Just like that."

Jeri snapped, did a quick turn, and fist-bumped the gloves. "She said she felt like our paths would cross again. She was all in, I'm telling you."

They all turned to Nelly. She immediately started scratching her arms.

"I hosted Grey in my house," Nelly began. "She asked if she could come up, and Biggie and Miss Jay approved it. She saw nuts scattered all over the place. Grey complimented my home and couldn't get over all the nuts everywhere. I told her that it hadn't always been easy for me, but I'd worked out arrangements and was very fortunate. She agreed." The nervous squirrel stuttered through her report, glad to have it behind her. She hoped she was done.

"And the possum?" the widow asked.

"I handled the possum," replied Jack. "I dropped her

on the Hangover Hedge and came straight here. She was an empty shell. She played possum as they passed by. She's a clear sign of what happens when someone says no to you, boss."

"What now?" Jeri was eager to know. "What's our next move?"

"It's time for me to go see Grey," the Widow calmly replied.

"Just you?" Jeri whined, clearly devastated. "What about us?"

The Widow could tell that Jeri wanted to play a key role in scoring the next big deal. "Just me and the Hourglass," the Widow confirmed. "This is *our* war."

The Hourglass beamed.

42

Chapter Forty-Two
The Puzzle Piece

Grey couldn't shake the visual of the possum. Or the feeling that there was a piece missing. She needed to know what it was.

"Guys, I need to know how these puzzle pieces fit together. Biggie, Jeri, Nelly, the Missing Missus. How is everyone linked? What am I missing?"

Biggie remained quiet. That was a first.

Grey watched Miss Jay let out a deep sigh. It looked like she'd been dreading this moment.

"There was a Black Widow who moved into the Jam Barn before you were born," Miss Jay reluctantly explained. "She was just a baby. Much smaller than any Widow I'd ever seen. She crawled in through a crack in the back of the barn and went straight for a spot of jam that had leaked from a jar. The Widow must have been terribly hungry. The second she tasted the jam, this bright red glow lit up the entire barn. It took a minute to figure out that the glow was actually coming from the Widow's back. That's when I first noticed the Hourglass."

Miss Jay took a deep breath and continued on. "I couldn't make out the exact words, but from a distance, it sounded like the Hourglass was pushing her. It told her she could take whatever she wanted. Then it rotated on her back and shot a red laser at one of Miss B's jam jars. The glass broke into a million little pieces and jam went everywhere. It was like a bomb had gone off. I was terrified. The Widow consumed everything. She didn't leave a single drop of jam. Broken glass lay all over the floor. The Widow ate all night while the Hourglass laughed at its first victory. By dawn, it had convinced her to build a web in the back of the barn.

"The Widow acted like she had something to prove. We couldn't tell whether the Widow or the Hourglass was in charge, but they both sought control over everything around them. It started with the cockroaches. Then, she started to get rid of the grasshoppers. The ants were next. We all felt that the Widow's push for control wouldn't stop with the ants. The Hourglass watched everyone in the barn. It was shaping up to be a hostile takeover." Miss Jay shuddered. Grey watched as Miss Jay fluffed up her feathers, gathering herself for what she was to say next.

"Grey, you have to understand. The Jam Barn is my home. I felt it was my duty to step up and protect our community. So," Miss Jay said quietly, "I orchestrated a coup. Woodie pretended to be asleep while the ants formed a line that led Miss B directly to the Widow's web. Miss B freaked out. She headed straight for a broom . . . maybe something even worse. We could all see it in Miss B's eyes. She intended to get rid of that spider for good. I saw the Widow dart for the door and assumed that she never looked back and never thought of us again.

"I now realize that the Widow and the Hourglass retreated to the Woodshed. They established the Worker's Decree and started enlisting animals on the farm to work for them. They've recruited Jack, Jeri, Nelly, and the Missing Missus. I don't know how much of this is the Widow and how much is the Hourglass. I don't know what happened to the Widow before she ran into our barn that day. I wish I'd taken the time to find out. Though now, I don't know if it would have made a difference."

Biggie had been listening intently. "You did what you had to do to preserve the safety of the barn," he assured Miss Jay. She looked at him with a worried glance.

"Yes, and that's what I felt in the moment. But looking back on it now, if I hadn't orchestrated the ants' march, then the Widow wouldn't have been forced to leave with such rage. There might be no Worker's Decree, and the Widow probably wouldn't have sought you out. Each action informed the next. See it as a picture developing around us. So Grey, to answer your question, it's me. I'm your missing puzzle piece. I'm afraid I might be the reason for all of this."

43

Chapter Forty-Three
The Greatest Greeter

Elaine the Butterfly saw the trio come around the corner. She was beside herself. She loved greeting a guest for the first time. She could look at a guest's face and see the second they took their first breath of air up here. It tasted different. Lighter. Sacred.

Elaine couldn't take it anymore. She bounced from

rock to rock and fluttered right up to plant a big kiss on Grey's cheek.

"Hey, hey, hey! I'm Elaine! Otherwise known as the most amazing, greatest greeter of all time. I've been personally chosen by Bo the Wise Owl to guard the gate and welcome all guests to the Lone Star Lodge. The Lodge is Bo's personal hideaway up here with Mr. and Mrs. Pine."

Elaine watched her guests laugh and applaud as she flew in loops around them. With her wings fully spread, she was pure energy. She knew her spirit was contagious. She saw that Grey was mesmerized, totally soaking it all up.

"It—it looks like you've been painted!" Grey finally sputtered.

Elaine loved attention. Her orange wings had black stripes on each side. The edges of her wings were lined with white polka dots. The same dots covered her face like freckles. She landed on Biggie's empty antler. Elaine started posing for imaginary cameras until she couldn't keep a straight face. She then took a dramatic bow, as if concluding a performance.

"The patterns came with the wings, but that's a story I'll have to tell you some other time. They're so awesome, right? Who doesn't love polka dots! And

I think the three ladies can agree that stripes make you look super cool," Elaine noted, motioning to both Grey and Miss Jay.

"I'm beyond thrilled to finally meet you, Grey. I can't wait for you to see the Lodge! If you're ready, I'll lead the way."

As Elaine flew ahead, she glanced over at Biggie. He was one of those friends that she might not see for years but could jump back into conversation with as though it had only been five minutes. She knew how precious and rare those friends were. "How was the trip?"

"Complicated," warned the deer. "We ran into Jeri on the first trail, and not by accident. Nothing ever is, though, right?"

44

Chapter Forty-Four
Lone Star Lodge

As they walked along the trail, Grey studied every detail.

Large rocks lay at equal distances on each side of the road. Ore rock after ore rock created a clear boundary for the path ahead. Grey looked up at the trees bending their branches in a canopy above her. She felt like she was walking through a hidden tunnel.

Grey noticed that the red dirt road paved itself as they walked along. With each step forward, it smoothed out, guaranteeing a sturdy step. Everything around her was working to ensure she arrived. She'd never felt safer than in this moment.

That's when Grey noticed that Elaine had stopped along the trail. It felt like the moment just before the curtain lifted for a big reveal on the Phoenix Club stage. This was the drumroll before the big moment.

And there it was. At first glance, it appeared to be a box of mirrors, miraculously hanging between two trees. The trees seemed to go up forever. She couldn't even see the top. She'd never seen trees that tall before.

"May I present Lone Star Lodge, and Mr. and Mrs. Pine," offered Elaine quietly, speaking with so much respect that she could barely form the words.

Grey stared ahead. She felt like she was solving a really hard riddle. Then it came to her. It was like watching nature's greatest symphony, with each of the individual pieces playing its part in a grand performance. She felt chills as her fur stood straight up. She could only assume that this happened to everyone the first time they saw Lone Star Lodge.

Lone Star Lodge was a glass house. It was designed to reflect its exterior surroundings. It had been built to camouflage its very existence. Every aspect of nature contributed to its success. Even the steps leading into the Lodge were extensions of Mr. and Mrs. Pine. Their roots held Lone Star Lodge firmly in place on the mountain's edge, which dangled somewhere between the earth and above.

45

Chapter Forty-Five
In a Flash

Grey's mind was blown. There was so much to take in.

As they passed through the front door, Grey heard Bo the Wise Owl. It sounded like his words moved in slow motion. They were rich, smooth, and commanding . . . but kind. They felt like the warm morning sun in those first few seconds when she stepped outside of the barn. His words felt like those moments, when she'd rather stay right there and let the sunshine swallow her whole before she spent one second in the shade.

"Well, look what the cat dragged in," Bo laughed upon seeing Biggie, Elaine, Grey, and Miss Jay enter Lone Star Lodge.

Grey was still hovering in the Wipi cup when Bo followed with, "It's nice to meet you, Grey. It's safe to come out. Please, have a look around."

She stepped out of the cup and nervously acknowledged her host. "Thank you, Mr. Bo," she replied as she jumped to the ground. She was completely overwhelmed by the owl's presence and the elaborate space before her.

Upon closer observation, Grey noticed that the glass walls were more than just walls. Aerial maps flicked past on the glass panels. The maps reminded Grey of the stars in the sky during the unplugged sessions at the pond. If these were stars, Grey couldn't make any sense of them.

Mr. and Mrs. Pine's height placed the Lodge at the highest possible elevation. From this height, Bo could see in all directions: north, south, east, and west. Grey felt a higher power here, too. It wasn't just a sensory overload. It felt very . . . specific. Every single thing had a purpose. A reason, perhaps. It made even the air taste powerful.

Grey didn't know where to look first, and she couldn't keep up with the speed of the flashing images on the glass walls. She didn't understand how to read anything, and she suddenly felt very dizzy. Grey wasn't sure if she felt dizzy because of the height or the constant blinking lights. It was too much to absorb. And then everything went dark.

46

Chapter Forty-Six
The Ringmaster

The Widow knew it would be a long walk to reach Grey. There were no words to express her dread. She reluctantly accepted her part in this mess. She'd accidentally given the Hourglass control over her life on that fateful day at the Jam Barn. She was forced to put on a brave face as the Hourglass demanded other animals do the same. The Hourglass was the ringleader, the circus master. Did that make her a clown?

That's not to say she didn't admire most of the clowns. Jack was a lost cause well before they met him, and the fox had always been a two-faced phony. But the old squirrel was a mother. She had to survive for her family. The Hourglass had been especially cruel to exploit Nelly. It was heartbreaking to watch the squirrel's new nervous ticks.

The point of no return had been Penelope the Possum, or the Missing Missus. That was the Widow's "a-ha" moment. Penelope had done nothing wrong. She was a star in the making. That was her only flaw in the eyes of the Hourglass: it saw her as a threat. It couldn't handle the thought of sharing the spotlight. To Penelope's credit, she fought back. She was determined to make it on her own. The Widow remembered that day as clearly as the day she herself had fallen prey to the Hourglass's spell.

"But, Penelope, what if you fail?" the Hourglass had taunted. "Wouldn't you like to have that extra bit of assurance, the net that will catch you and make sure failure isn't an option? What if you're just not good enough?"

"I don't ask myself those questions," Penelope had immediately countered. "I ask, 'What if you succeed?' It drives me to make the day count. I know in my heart that I can and should be the closing act."

The Widow was sickened when the Hourglass broke Penelope. From that moment on, the Widow pushed herself to perform, just like the rest of the recruits. They were all playing possum in some way. She just had the extra weight of the Hourglass on her back.

The Hourglass lit their path up the mountain. It decided which trail to take. It rewarded the Widow for staying on track and following its lead. It didn't allow her to think for herself anymore, and she didn't dare reveal that she still wanted to. The Hourglass's chatter was constant whether she responded or not.

Be the closing act.

47

Chapter Forty-Seven
Love Letters

Mr. and Mrs. Pine had a fairy-tale love story. They'd grown up together, learned together, and planted a family together. They wanted to build a legacy of hard work and commitment.

Mr. Pine was a romantic. For as long as Mrs. Pine could remember, Mr. Pine had written her love letters. Some letters celebrated special occasions. He wrote other letters just because. Mr. Pine claimed that his letters had inspired *The Buzzy Bark.* The weekly paper was Mrs. Pine's love letter to the BMF community. Mrs. Pine wanted the animals to know they were never alone. She wanted them to applaud each other's accomplishments. Mrs. Pine knew the paper would build a connection between animals who might not meet in real life.

Despite their growth over the years, *The Buzzy Bark* writing room was still Mrs. Pine's favorite space. She edited every single page in that room. The bees often joked that that's where the magic happened.

48

Chapter Forty-Eight
Under Pressure

Bo saw Mrs. Pine from every window. He could see her laugh lines and wrinkles, those deep-set crinkles that she'd earned so gracefully with time. He saw the curves of her branches and the humble nature in which she greeted guests as they arrived. He laughed to himself as he saw her fidget. Mrs. Pine was many things, but patient had never been one of them. Good thing patience was his specialty.

Bo watched and waited. He'd seen many animals faint from the onset of pressure at the top. He knew Grey just needed a minute. He smiled at the sight of her curled up in a ball sleeping on the sofa. He'd never seen a cat more destined for a couch.

As they waited, Miss Jay looked to the wise owl for clarity.

"Why Grey? Mr. and Mrs. Pine sent word at her birth that I was to be her guardian, but they never told me why. I know she's special. I understand the circumstances. But what's her gift? What did you see?"

Bo opened his mouth to answer, and the sleeping cat began to stir.

WELCOME GREX

49

Chapter Forty-Nine
Lounging Like a House Cat

Grey's head felt fuzzy. She wondered if it had all been a dream. She heard voices and laughter, and she felt the most amazing breeze blow over her. The Jam Barn didn't have breezes like that.

Grey slowly raised her head, blinking away the confusion. She immediately remembered where she was and who she had met. Bo. The Lodge. Mr. and Mrs.

Pine. The Widow. The Hourglass. It all came flooding back like a movie playing on repeat in her mind.

Grey noticed a winding staircase that led to another floor above them. She felt a comfy couch underneath her and noticed they were all sitting in a lounge. As she looked around, she realized the Lodge had four different lounges. Each one faced a different direction. This helped Bo watch the maps and events happening below. Large stars with letters—"N," "S," "E," or "W"—floated near the ceiling in each room. The group knew they faced north because the "N" star floated near the ceiling in their lounge.

Grey heard a lot of sounds while she observed the inside of the Lodge. She finally found the source of the noise. The glass walls had disappeared in the north-facing lounge, and there were animals and nests gathered everywhere around them. It looked like a carnival had been set up outside. Grey suddenly felt like a spotlight shone down on her. These animals had all come to see her for themselves.

Mr. and Mrs. Pine pointed and waved their pine needles back and forth to say "hello." Grey could see that they were overwhelmed with joy.

"Hi, Grey!" Mrs. Pine shouted. "We've been waiting for you! Well, *I've* been waiting. And watching. I'm actually the one who named you! You can thank me later. You're as beautiful now as the day you were born."

Mrs. Pine gushed, and Grey blushed.

Elaine led the redbirds through a welcome song while the hummingbirds zoomed in and out to catch a glimpse of the cat.

The squirrels had memorized an official line dance and stood in even rows on three huge branches. In unison, they stepped forward and back, forward and back. One arm up, two arms up, cross over, and turn. Shake the tail, clap, turn, and repeat. The dance reminded her of the chickens at the Phoenix Club. Grey decided that the Lodge residents were amazing.

Even the bees took a break from distributing *The Buzzy Bark* so they could join the fun. Grey sensed that this was a rare occasion for them. They put forth so much effort. A few of the bees made a batch of homemade buzzy punch and passed out cups for everyone. The rest of the beehive flew by with a "Welcome Grey" sign they'd made out of old copies of *The Buzzy Bark*.

Grey heard Bo's deep laugh.

"Grey, there was no way I could keep these guys waiting any longer. I knew the breeze and fresh air would help settle you. I can open and close the glass anytime you need to take a break. Maybe say a quick hello before I raise it back up?"

Grey sat up, smiling, and waved at her new friends. She felt such love here, and she was so grateful for their friendly faces.

With the welcoming party winding down, Bo turned to Grey. "You'll have plenty of opportunities to meet everyone after," he said with a kind smile. He acknowledged the rest of the group. "Okay, everyone. We've got to get to work in here. Keep your eyes on the trails. The others arrive tomorrow."

Grey wondered what Bo meant when he said "after." She also wondered who else they were expecting. These thoughts floated through her mind for a second, but she lost her train of thought as the glass moved, sealing the room and locking them in place.

Chapter Fifty

The Glasses That See All

Grey observed Bo. She saw a gentleness in the large, yellow eyes behind the big glasses. She got the sense that those eyes preferred to see life's great potential. Grey wanted to know everything about Bo.

"Is it true that you can see all?" Grey asked. "Even the future?" Grey looked over at Biggie as he sat on one of the couches in the lounge. "Biggie said that you function at a different frequency than the other animals. What does that even mean?"

Miss Jay cleared her throat, interrupting Grey's stream of questions. "Grey!" she scolded, standing up from where she sat on an armchair. "It's impolite to ask someone so many questions at once!"

Bo extended a large wing toward Miss Jay, who sat back down. "It's quite all right," he said with a chuckle. Bo nodded his head to Grey's questions. "I do see all, and I don't take that power lightly. Would you like me to explain, Grey?"

Grey sat up to better understand every detail. "Yes," she said, eager to finally learn how the owl worked.

"They call me a Great Horned Owl, which is amusing. I don't actually have horns," he explained. He pointed a talon at his head. Grey was surprised to see two tufted feathers where horns should have been. The feathers just *looked* like horns. "My brown, speckled feathers—much like my home—camouflage me. I completely blend in with my surroundings. The edges of my wings help me fly silently. When I do have to leave Lone Star Lodge, no one can hear me.

"My vision is a gift. I believe that gifts should only be used for good. I have to protect my gift. In doing so, I keep everyone safe. There are a lot of animals out there who would like to use my eyes for the wrong reasons, but they can't get to Lone Star Lodge. Everyone here works together to guard this place." Bo paused as Grey looked around at the walls of the Lodge. She studied the glass windows, the compasses, and even the pedestal Bo stood on.

"I designed the Lodge to face all directions. When I stand in the center, I can move anywhere and determine the areas of most importance. I can actually almost turn my head all the way around. This helps me scan nearly the entire space without moving my body."

Grey watched as Bo demonstrated. He looked almost all the way around the room. His body stayed in one place. She had a hunch that this move never failed to impress his guests. "Cool party trick," she acknowledged enviously. The group laughed as Grey tried to copy Bo.

"Everyone always tries," Bo smirked. "And everyone always fails," he said, winking. She watched closely as Bo pointed to the blinking images on the glass. She leaned in, hanging on his every word.

"I created these maps to show space, distance, and souls," he continued. "I believe that every animal has a soul. Some call it their gut. Maybe your soul is that feeling in your stomach when you're close to an answer. Maybe it's that inner voice that dings when you know something, but you aren't sure how you know it. Our souls often reflect the most honest version of who we really are. They're all connected.

"So, by factoring in space, distance, and souls, my maps reveal the path ahead. I'm farsighted, so it's easier for me to look down the road at the long-distance view. When it's time to focus on the present moment, my glasses help me zoom in."

Grey watched as Bo tapped his glasses to zoom for effect. She had a feeling they were always ready in the blink of an eye.

"Like my wings, these glasses are designed to tune in to the situations that need attention now. The maps forecast the future, but the glasses see all."

51

Chapter Fifty-One
Cautionary Tales

Bo flew to the sofa to sit beside Grey.

"The Black Widow sent a troop of cautionary tales your way, all to prove a point. Any idea what it was?" he asked.

"Sure. She and the Hourglass wanted me to know that they're in control."

"Actually, no. That's the message they had hoped to

deliver. But it's not the point they actually made. That's one of the things I'm here to help you see. The fox and the squirrel were supposed to demonstrate what the Widow and Hourglass can give their workers. The Missing Missus, on the other hand, outright declined to sign the Worker's Decree. They placed her on your path to show you what happens when someone says no to the Widow and the Hourglass. Here's the thing, though. None of these cautionary tales matter. Have you figured out why?"

Bo saw Grey pause. She was reluctant to admit that she didn't know the answer.

"No, Bo, I haven't figured out why," Grey said quietly.

"The Black Widow has her own story," Bo shared. "Her truth. You have yours. Your stories overlap in her misplaced trust of the Hourglass and its quest for control. You need to focus on your story. Your purpose. Find that, and you find your answer."

Bo looked over at Miss Jay and Biggie, who had both been listening quietly. He paused to see if they had anything to add.

Miss Jay sat up. "The way someone reacts to a situation says more about them than it does about you," offered Miss Jay. "Because they dropped Jeri, Nelly, and the Missing Missus in your path, we learned that the

Widow or the Hourglass felt they needed reinforcements. It said more about them and their insecurities than it did about their workers. Silence would have been much louder."

"Very true," Bo agreed. "Remember that no one chose the Widow. They chose the only answer they could see because they weren't looking to themselves as a solution. Your decision has to be based on your story, not someone else's."

Biggie finally spoke. "Grey, the Widow isn't your problem. No one has power over you until you allow them to take it. Take that lesson from me; I have the battle wound. It might be a different scene, but it's a classic tale. You have to look inside yourself if you want to see a different outcome."

Grey looked at Biggie, but she didn't see wounds: she saw light. "That's not a scar," she countered. "It's a medal. And you didn't just survive, you thrived. You're the Widow's cautionary tale fail."

Bo's heart felt so full, it could burst.

Chapter Fifty-Two

The Hoo Game

Bo glided down the staircase as he returned to the north lounge with renewed energy. He had run to gather materials. He removed his glasses. Bo had an unmistakable twinkle in his eyes. "Let's play a game," he suggested to the group.

Grey laughed. "I love games. Can't wait to beat you at your own," she dared playfully.

"It's called the Hoo Game," Bo explained. "It's a game of questions. You write down the first thing that pops into your mind after I ask a question. I'm giving each of you an old copy of *The Buzzy Bark* to write on, and one of Mrs. Pine's pens to write down your answers. The pens are made out of ink-dipped pine needles from Mrs. Pine herself. They will only write the truth. Mrs. Pine designed them that way. Because she's a Loblolly Pine Tree, she named them her "lobipens." He paused, giving the group a second to get situated.

Biggie stood up. Bo knew instantly that his game had been derailed, but at least they were in for a show.

Biggie started with leg stretches. Totally unnecessary leg stretches. He walked all around the room. Arm punches came next. Biggie looked like a boxer preparing for a big match. He ducked and squatted. His massive body barely fit in the crowded lounge. Bo had no choice but to wait this one out. *Perhaps I should change the name of the game to "Hoo Doesn't Love Biggie"*, he mused to himself. After fifteen minutes of watching Biggie physically prepare for a three-question game, they could finally proceed. Bo shook his head and laughed. He had to get Grey back on track.

"Now, for the first question: what makes you happy?" Bo asked the group. "Forget about whether your answer is right or wrong. Just write down whatever pops into your mind." The other three animals paused, thoughtful looks falling over their faces. They scribbled down their answers around the same time. Bo waited until they had all put their lobipens down.

"Second question: how do you honor that? Meaning, what activity do you do on any given day to feel happy?" This question took the trio a while to answer. Grey looked up, lost in thought. Her concentrated face made Bo smile.

"And lastly, how would you describe yourself?"

Biggie tried to peek over Miss Jay's shoulder to look at her answers. Miss Jay saw him looking and promptly flew onto a nearby bookshelf, taking her answers with her. Bo noticed that Grey seemed to be overthinking the questions. He wasn't surprised.

"Miss Jay, would you mind sharing what you wrote down?" Bo asked his friend. He knew he could count on her for a solid answer. Biggie, not so much. Bo thought back to the leg stretches and arm punches.

"I'm happiest when I'm home, making the rounds to

see my friends, and taking care of the Jam Barn," Miss Jay offered. "I never miss my meetings with Woodie or the wildflowers. I'd describe myself as a community leader. I'm sensitive to those around me, and I think of myself as the keeper of the peace at BMF."

"Perfect!" Bo praised. "And, Biggie, I'm truly scared to ask, but what did you actually write down?" he inquired.

"I'm glad you asked, Bo," Biggie said seriously. "I'm happiest on the front porch at Station II, a little Mango Moonshine in hand, watching a sky full of stars." He was telling the truth, bless his heart. It was definitely funny enough to warrant a chuckle from the crowd.

"To answer your third question, I'd describe myself as real. I'm just a good ole deer who found my real strength after losing my false sense of it. It took a long time at the Lodge to appreciate that strength."

They all stared at Biggie. You just never knew with him. And, yet, there it was: Biggie at his "most real." Bo applauded his beloved deer while Biggie took a bow. A massive, occupy-the-entire-room bow.

"Grey, I think your magic lies in owning who you are," Bo surmised. "Or, as I like to say, 'hoo' you are. I knew my reason for being here early on in my life. I was lucky. I oversee the connection we all have to one another. I help those who are ready to do the real work to reach the top. For me, the 'top' simply means the best version of yourself. It means you have a sense of purpose and the confidence to claim it. Reaching the top doesn't have anything to do with your status, or your stripes, or your rack." He saw Biggie smile.

"I think everyone should have a shot at finding their hoo, but I don't believe in free admission. If you make it inside my gate, it's because I've seen your potential."

53

Chapter Fifty-Three
The Spinning Wheel

Grey watched as Bo left the room. He had suggested a short break. Grey needed a minute to think about her answers. She walked over to the glass walls. She knew she was close to an epiphany. Like the maps on the glass, she could feel the answers to Bo's three questions blinking around her.

Grey felt like she'd been running on a wheel that couldn't stop. She wasn't sure the wheel went anywhere, either. Her story and the Widow's story were intertwined. Grey was starting to see the faint circle of cause and effect. Realization dawned on the little cat. She needed to find Bo.

54

Chapter Fifty-Four
Door with No Doorknob

Grey left Miss Jay and Biggie in the lounge as she went looking for Bo. She found him waiting patiently at the bottom of the winding staircase.

"After you," Bo nodded, motioning for her to lead him to the top floor. As she reached the top of the stairs, she saw two doors: one on the right, and one on the left.

"Turn left," Bo directed.

Grey immediately noticed two things about the door on the left. First, it was painted a shade of purple that reminded her of the wisteria from the Hangover Hedge. Second, it had no doorknob. She noticed two arrows on the door, one short and one long. The arrows sat safely tucked inside a ring. The arrows pointed at the ground; they appeared to be sleeping. She watched as Bo gently tapped each of them awake with one talon.

"Are we late?" the long arrow shrieked as it sprung to life. He was panicked that he'd overslept and missed a deadline. The other arrow woke a little slower, blinking as he took in the new guest.

"Not at all. Just hold tight," Bo responded as he turned to Grey.

"When the time is right, I want you to move the arrows on the ring. Move them anywhere you wish; they must reflect the exact moment. Only *you* can know that exact moment because it's relative. By that, I mean the concept of time is relative. I've been here for years and years and years, yet it feels like seconds to me. You embarked on this journey only a few short days ago, yet I'm sure it feels like decades have passed.

"Remember downstairs, when I said that your magic lies within? This door will unlock your magic. This is the trick to the Hoo Game. There is a prize waiting inside, and it's just for you. But, to collect your prize and finish the game, you have to open a door. You'll know when the time is right."

Grey stared at the purple door for what felt like hours. For reasons unknown to her, and with a certainty that she could not explain, she moved the short arrow to the number eight. She then guided the long arrow all the way around the ring, making a full loop before landing at the six. The arrows called out, "Eight-thirty!". Grey heard a soft, buzzing alarm.

The purple door with no doorknob clicked open. It invited her and her alone inside. Bo stood back and motioned with his wing for her to go ahead. The door wasn't the only thing that had just clicked open.

55

Chapter Fifty-Five
The Bonded Word

Grey felt like she was entering a private space. She heard buzzing all around her.

It took a moment for her eyes to adjust as she walked into the room. As she found her bearings, she realized the walls were covered with pages of *The Buzzy Bark.*

Paper covered every inch of the walls. There must have been hundreds of pages. Grey wondered if they had any specific order to them. Even if there was an order, she didn't know what it was. Just then, Grey noticed something very curious. The pages had no stories on them. Not a single word. They just had the name of the publication on the top left side. That's when Grey noticed the tables in the center of the room, and the lobipens. They tapped impatiently on the tables. They seemed to be waiting for something. It sounded like the room was filled with drums.

"Hello?" Grey called out to anyone who might hear her. "I'm here." She watched as the lobipens bounced up from their rhythmic beat. They turned away from the tables and clamored for a free spot on the wall. One winner squeezed through the masses to write "I'm here" on the first page in a row of pages. The lobipen looked like it had won a hard-fought race, pausing to catch its breath. *What is happening?* Grey thought.

"Am I supposed to say something specific?" she asked, and watched again as the lobipens fought and pushed for coverage of the newly spoken line.

This is crazy. What are they doing? Grey thought as she started to back toward the purple door. Then she had an epiphany. Would the pens do *anything* she said?

"Fall to the ground," she ordered. She watched in amazement as the lobipens all flicked once and fell to the floor.

Grey switched gears. "Crumple them," she demanded as she looked at the pages on the wall. She stood in awe as the neatly arranged pages curled up in balls. *How am I doing that?* her inner dialogue continued.

If her words could drop the pens and crumple the paper, what else could they do? Could they move the tables? She had to try it. This was getting very cool, very fast.

"Flip the tables," she said out loud, testing the strength of her power. She watched as all of the tables flipped onto their sides.

Grey had barely processed the mess she'd made of the room when a tiny bee darted toward her. Grey jumped for cover, cowering behind a flipped table.

She heard the bee laughing hysterically at her very uncool and uncatlike move. Grey looked down and saw that her tail stuck straight out. *Real smooth,* she thought. She began to laugh, too. A lot. It felt so good to laugh. Grey remembered the day Miss Jay told her how important it was to laugh at herself.

"You must be Grey," the bee said after she regained her composure. "I'm Laura, Special Reporter for *The*

Buzzy Bark, and, more importantly, Mrs. Pine's right-hand man. Well, bee."

Grey tried to collect herself as she stood back up. "Nice to meet you, Laura. This might be a strange question, but do you know what's happening here?" she asked the friendly bee.

"Well, for starters, you've made a mess, and you'll have to clean it up," Laura laughed. "But on the bright side, you've also just unlocked the power of your voice. Your words have magic now. Special power. You released it when you positioned the arrows. It was your time. The click you heard when the door opened was your awakening. It wasn't the clock's."

"Come again?" Grey was confused.

Laura shifted her approach. "Let me put it a bit differently. Bo's magic lies in his ability to see. His vision. Your magic lies in your voice. You can now do anything with your words. They can protect you and work for you. They can break things or build things. They're bonded to you. However, they can also help others. That's your trick. For those reasons, you'll always need to choose your words very carefully and keep your voice safe. Your words can do anything as long as they are used for good. Consider them a portal to your power."

It took every ounce of energy in Grey's body to stay calm, cool, and collected. "Thank you for explaining that to me, Laura," she managed to mutter.

"That's what I'm here for," Laura smiled. "Well, that's part of what I'm here for, anyway. Stay tuned for more, as I always say. May I suggest you take a minute to let the news soak in? Pun intended."

Grey laughed absentmindedly. Her mind was racing. She had a magic voice! Seriously?! This was the answer she'd been looking for, for as long as she could remember. It seemed like forever. Grey wondered if forever was relative, too. Either way, her words were her power. Now, she just needed a plan.

Chapter Fifty-Six

Writing's on the Wall

Grey decided to go for a walk. She needed to think. She walked down the front steps of the Lodge and made her way to the mountain's edge. It was quiet there. She could hear the trees whispering amongst themselves. Other than that, it was very still. Grey sat on the edge of the mountain. The sun was setting. She had never seen anything more beautiful.

Grey had seen three cautionary tales on her hike. Her instincts told her that meeting Jeri, Nelly, and the Missing Missus meant change was coming. She knew that the animals would talk about her response to the Widow and her Worker's Decree. Grey's choices would set in motion a reaction. She finally understood what Miss Jay meant when she said that life came full circle. It was crystal clear to her now.

Grey felt her old insecurities rising. She thought back to when she wanted everyone to like her. She remembered her fear of failure. Her insecurities had been big. However, now Grey knew that they didn't have power over her anymore. Grey could release them just like she released her voice in the room behind the purple door.

"I thought that if I looked good enough or sounded smart enough, then everything would somehow fall into place," she said to herself. "I wanted the other animals to validate my ambition. But now I know that it doesn't work that way." She felt the gentle breeze of confirmation from the trees around her.

Grey turned around and looked at the Lodge. The breeze had carried her words. They wrote themselves on the glass walls. She was looking at a reflection of her voice, a voice she now felt empowered to use.

"I need to rise above the Widow's Hourglass. I need to rise above the ego in all of us," she said aloud, to no one in particular. "I need to go high."

Grey watched as specific words continued writing themselves on the glass walls like run-on sentences. "Rise," "High," "Rise," "High," "Rise," "High," "Rise." This was her map, and only she could see it. She knew why Mr. and Mrs. Pine had sent Miss Jay to be her guardian. She knew what Bo had seen. She knew her potential role in all of this.

She had waited her whole life to feel like she was home. She wanted to wake up like Miss Jay and know that she was exactly where she was supposed to be. Grey hadn't felt that way yet. Somehow, in that very moment, she knew the reason.

Home was a space within. It's wasn't a place. It was a mindset. All she had to do was stand up and claim it. Her home. Her voice. Her hoo. That's what Bo wanted. It's also what her brother had wanted. Bob wasn't trying to be rude when he said that he couldn't wait to see who she would become. Like Bo, Bob was simply waiting for Grey to finally speak up on her own behalf.

Grey walked back to the Lodge as the sky grew darker. She felt strong and steady. She was confident in who she'd just become. Grey knew her brother would be proud. That knowledge motivated her even more. Just as the Lodge reflected the collective power of nature, it also reflected the collective benefit of her gift. The battle between Grey and the Widow wasn't a battle for control. It was a battle for identity. Even though this was Grey's story, it would lay a path for the animals who followed.

She smiled. The answer to the Hoo Game, and to all of this, was suddenly so simple.

57

Chapter Fifty-Seven
The Chosen One

Grey was still smiling as she walked up the front steps of the Lodge. As she opened the front door, however, she sensed a drastic change among her group. Grey knew that Bo was expecting the Widow. She felt the answer before she asked, and, as a result, she directed her question solely to Bo.

"Is the Widow here yet?" she asked, knowing that

her question would also act as an answer for the wise owl. It would quietly confirm the clarity and peace of mind that Grey had just gained.

She watched as Bo's glasses settled and his eyes relaxed.

"Yes. She's outside the front gate," he confirmed. "She and the Hourglass are waiting for you to exit the Lodge."

Miss Jay, who had been noticeably upset, could no longer stay silent. "Do you know what you're going to do? Are you going to refuse the Decree? Do you have a plan? Have you made a decision? We're all going with you. We'll fight the Widow and the Hourglass together. I'm sure they want to settle a score with me. This was all my fault anyway."

Grey raised her paws and motioned for Miss Jay to stop talking. "Miss Jay, don't you know that it's impolite to ask someone so many questions at once?" she asked with a wink. "I'm going alone. I was chosen for this, and yes, I know what to do. I'm ready."

58

Chapter Fifty-Eight
Under the Radar

The Widow sat very still under the heat of the Hourglass's red light. It was the light of arrogance and ego gone wrong. The Widow wished she could leave. She longed for someplace quiet and under the radar. She didn't want to listen to the Hourglass's nonstop chatter anymore.

As they waited for Grey to leave the Lodge, the

Widow looked up to the stars. She looked for a light that could outshine the glow of anger riding on her back.

Chapter Fifty-Nine

Strike Out

Grey knew the Hourglass was waiting. It would see her coming through the darkness, alone. She wanted it that way.

Grey walked to the gate with her head held high, waiting patiently. The quiet felt like the calm before the storm. The slow creak of the swinging gate sounded like a siren in the silence. She wanted it that way, too.

Grey saw the line where the Lodge ended and the rest of the mountain began. The line where Bo's protection stopped, and her own strength would need to step in. This was the line she needed to cross. It was drawn clearly in the sand.

Grey felt the heat of the Hourglass before she saw it. The red ore looked even redder under its furious glare. She could also feel eyes on her, even though they were all hidden. The squirrels, the grasshoppers, the ants, the birds, the bees: they were all watching. She even felt Bob and Shi. They were all waiting for her. Waiting to see what she really stood for. Waiting to see who she'd become. Waiting for the showdown. She now understood that they were all prepared to fight with her, not against her. They were there to protect her, as she would protect them. The other animals needed her to find her voice as much as she did. Her voice would provide a platform for many to come.

Grey followed the red glow until she stood firmly in front of the Widow. The Hourglass shook violently with a venomous hate. It was ready to fire. It was ready to dominate. She knew that the Widow wasn't. Grey could see it in her eyes. She remembered the direction that had been written on the glass walls: "Rise High." Grey knew the Hourglass had no power over her. She raised her head and spoke in its direction, not the Widow's.

"Shield me," Grey instructed her voice.

Grey paused long enough for the Hourglass to aim and fire. She knew it would strike. Her voice formed a shield, a barrier that the Hourglass couldn't penetrate. She felt the laser fly by, redirected. A failed shot. The Hourglass's aim wasn't off, but its weapon stood no chance in the battle for her identity.

Grey spoke directly to the Widow. "I thought I was supposed to represent accomplishment." The Hourglass shot another laser; it bounced right off Grey's shield. "I thought I'd find happiness once I'd proven myself. That wasn't the case. That wasn't my purpose." Another shot flew by. Grey could sense the Hourglass's frustration, but she still spoke only to the Widow. "I was chosen so that I could use my voice and pay it forward. For me. For you. For everyone. I'm an example of what's possible through forgiveness and fortitude. I'm here to reroute our connection and close the loop of consequence between all of us. I'm the fresh start."

Her words echoed through the mountain and sent shockwaves into the air. Grey knew she inched closer to victory for all with each sentence. She chose her next words carefully. She looked directly into the Widow's eyes. She needed this moment to count.

"You've been in someone else's shadow for far too long. We both need to shake the weight from our shoulders. You deserve to be happy. Let me help you. Take my paw."

Grey watched as the Widow closed her eyes and took a deep breath. She reached for Grey's paw.

Grey raised her head and spoke in the Hourglass's direction once more.

"Shatter it," Grey demanded, once again of her voice.

Grey saw her words whip through the air like a tornado. With perfect precision, the swirling storm of love and acceptance shattered the Harrowing Hourglass into a thousand pieces. Grey saw the sands of their past dissolve into tomorrow's promise. Their shared pain fell through the earth like quicksand. The Widow could now speak for herself for what Grey assumed was the first time since her first fateful run to the Jam Barn.

Grey and the Widow stood very still. Grey looked at the new friend before her and smiled. "What's your name?" she asked.

60

Chapter Sixty

By Dawn's Early Light

The Widow could see Grey's mouth moving, but she couldn't hear anything Grey said. She was still dazed by the explosion. She felt ringing vibrations through her entire body. The Widow could feel eyes glued to her, watching and waiting for her next move.

"My name?" the Widow repeated the question to

herself. "I was never given a name. The Hourglass told me I was a Black Widow. That's all I've ever known. I guess you could say that's all I've ever been to anyone. What's in a name, anyway?" she shrugged, trying to sound more carefree than she really felt. She was still visibly shaken.

"As much or as little as you want there to be," responded Grey. "A name can mean everything to you, or it can mean nothing at all. That's for you to decide. A name can be symbolic or silly. Strong or safe. Significant or insignificant. Mrs. Pine named me Grey. Until today, I assumed my name had to do with the markings on my fur. Now, I believe my name represents balance."

"I wouldn't know how to choose a name," the Widow replied quietly.

"Well, you're strong, beautiful, and independent," said Grey. The Widow blushed. "Let's start there and celebrate that. You hold the power to empower yourself and others from this point forward. Embrace this opportunity to shine bright with a new day."

The Widow saw Grey pause. She watched as a huge smile covered the cat's face. "How do you feel about Dawn?" Grey asked. "It has a ring to it, don't you think?"

The Widow began to cry. She'd never cried before. She'd never felt safe enough to cry in front of someone else. She'd seen other animals cry in the Jam Barn late at night as the Hourglass watched them. But the Widow's tears were different. They were tears of joy. Tears of hope. With every fiber of her being, the Widow knew she'd just become Dawn.

61

Chapter Sixty-One
Fireworks

Shooting stars lit the entire sky, burning light from every possible direction. Grey stood beside Dawn and watched the show. Neither of them had ever seen anything like it.

"Now that we have a moment, do you mind if I express my gratitude?" Dawn asked. "Because of you, we both have an opportunity to show the world what we're really capable of."

Grey glanced at the widow and grinned. "Does that mean you'll join me at the Lodge? You knew I would ask."

"Not yet," Dawn replied. "You have unfinished business for yourself. You have work to do, and so do I."

"Why can't we do our work together?" Grey wondered.

Dawn laughed. It was the purest sound Grey had ever heard.

"We will work together," Dawn replied. "We'll do amazing things together when the time is right. As you said, this is the beginning of a new day. But first, we have to find our individual paths to greatness. I have all the faith in the world that our paths will cross again."

The two new friends stood together, old contracts fulfilled and new promises in place.

They watched as the stars aligned.

62

Chapter Sixty-Two
Monarch of Change

Grey walked back to the Lodge. She thought of the animals who had inspired her. She thought of the Phoenix Club. All of the animals worked together to create a special night each month. The frogs, who would probably go unrecognized, jumped from row to row to make sure that everyone had a good seat. The dogs dragged supplies from place to place. They were happy with a simple pat on the back. Without teamwork, those nights would never happen.

As she moved on to what was next, Grey knew she had to remember where she came from. She had to remember her roots and the friends she had made at Black Mountain Farm. Most of the animals here would never know their impact on her. Grey was lost in thought when Elaine suddenly appeared.

"You didn't think I was going to let you take the victory lap alone, did you?" the butterfly asked. "You're free as a bird! Or, wait, a butterfly. I meant butterfly. I don't know why the birds get all the credit. Anyway, tell me! Tell me the answer. I'm dying to know."

Grey was very confused. "The answer to what? Are you talking about the Hoo Game?"

"Nope, not at all. That's totally Bo's thing. I'm talking about the question in your own head right now. The one you'll ask yourself from this moment forward."

"Elaine, what makes you think you have any idea what's in my head?" Grey laughed.

"Because every guest reaches a point where it's the only question that remains. We're alone here, so you have nothing to lose by telling me. Come on, it's just ME." She emphasized the word "me" with a swirly loop through the sky, a move she pulled out only for special occasions. And special requests.

Grey marveled at the butterfly. She watched Elaine sing and dance and bop around. Grey slowly realized she had no clue as to what choices she'd had to make in life.

"Have you ever asked yourself the same question?" Grey cleverly redirected back to Elaine.

Elaine smiled. "Our circumstances were different. I had to fight my way out of a cocoon to survive. You think that barn down there is claustrophobic?" Elaine shuddered. "I always knew I was more than a caterpillar. I had to make big changes to transform into what you see today. But, in my heart, I knew I was a butterfly from the day I was born. So, to answer the question, I wanted to fly. I wanted to bring joy to others. I know firsthand that a smile goes a long way. Now, your turn. What do you want?"

Grey was just about to answer Elaine when she heard a roaring sound. She noticed that all of the trees stood at attention. In a display of respect and admiration, all of the Lodge residents lined the path and cheered as Grey returned. The applause could be heard for miles.

As Grey walked through the front door, Bo winked at her and whispered in her ear, "I saw that coming."

A smile goes
a long way.

63

Chapter Sixty-Three
Meeting with Destiny

Long ago, many years before Grey and Miss Jay and Biggie, there were only two rooms up on the mountain: her "writing" room with the purple door, and this one, which would become his. Bo reflected on that day every morning. He'd sat in this very chair, at this very table. Mrs. Pine had sat across from him.

He took a moment to look around his room and smile. It smiled back. Or at least, that's how he saw it. He kept his private collection of canvases up here. He painted the portraits from memory. His vision, and the essence of their answers to the Hoo Game. He'd captured each Lodge guest after they'd gone. It was his way of remembering them. Honoring them. This was his gallery to be still and to reflect on the gifts of many.

He'd known it was a tall ask. The tallest, actually. Nonetheless, he'd come prepared to pitch his idea. As it turned out, he didn't need to. The minute they'd met in this room, Bo and Mrs. Pine both knew the plan had been in place the whole time. He'd even heard Mrs. Pine later admit that she couldn't be sure *The Buzzy Bark* didn't start itself as a result of the foresight that Bo would come.

"What do you see for the future of *The Buzzy Bark*?" Bo had asked her.

"I want us to keep telling the truth," she'd answered, without missing a beat. "We're the heartbeat of the mountain. I always want to provide a space for honest storytelling. *The Buzzy Bark* is a straightforward report that encourages everyone to share their tales, support one another, and extend a helping hand."

Mrs. Pine had talked for hours about the nature

around them. She talked about the heroes behind her success. Her roots were held in place by the ore of the mountain. Ore provided the real stability. Her pine needles worked hard with the sun to convert the energy necessary to fuel her great height. Their special skills gave Mrs. Pine the idea to use the prickly needles as pens. The "lobipens" converted honest words into headline news for *The Buzzy Bark.*

"Our roots are strong here, but we can all feel a big change coming," she'd confided. "We need to branch out. In order to do so, we have to look ahead."

Mrs. Pine and Bo agreed right then to build Lone Star Lodge. It would be built to nurture animals who appeared on Bo's radar of unlimited potential. The Lodge would become a hidden gem, designed to bring out the magic inside special souls. It would only be accessible to animals who would share their gifts. The Lodge would become a space where action was a pure reflection of intention. That's when the idea had come to Bo.

"What do we do first?" Mrs. Pine had asked, unsure of where to start.

"We build a glass house," Bo replied.

Chapter Sixty-Four

A Picture's Worth a Thousand Words

Grey was celebrating with all of the Lodge residents when she saw Bo tilt his head in her direction. He wanted her to follow him. Grey made her way up the winding staircase. This time she turned right, toward a green door. As Bo led her inside, she realized that the door wasn't the only green thing. The whole room was green. But it wasn't the green that stopped her in her tracks: it was the paintings.

Two blue velvet chairs sat by a table. She watched as Bo politely relocated the chair he intended for her, positioning it for the best window view. He motioned for Grey to take the seat at the head of the table.

Grey was still taking in the paintings in the room. There were so many. They covered the walls, the ceiling; some even sat on the floor. "Who are they?" Grey asked, before she'd really even formed the thought for herself.

"Well, that's a question for them, and the point of the game, right?" he laughed.

"Yes, it is," Grey acknowledged as she smiled warmly at the portraits around her. It took her a second, but Grey got it. These were the faces before her. The previous guests. That's "hoo" they were. Bo captured their gifts and their spirit in the highest possible place and honored them with daily gratitude. His canvases were their success stories. Biggie's portrait showed a close up of that twinkle in his eyes. She could almost hear Biggie laughing in the room with them.

"After everything you've been through, I'd really love for you to tell me who you are," Bo requested. "I want to hear it from you, here, before you go, and in your own words. You can think of your answer as earning your place on my wall. After all, a picture's worth a thousand words," Bo grinned.

"I'm a scrappy barn cat with a gift," Grey replied without hesitation. "I love Black Mountain Farm, and it will always have a special place in my heart. I was brought to the farm because I can make a difference with the power of my voice. I know that that difference extends beyond the mountain and the farm. That's the aerial view on your maps. Zoom in a little closer with your glasses, at the good stuff, and you'll see I'm also a cat who likes to light the stage on fire and challenge the system. I am, after all, the one who shattered it."

Grey watched as Bo removed his glasses and placed them on the table directly in front of her. "Speaking of, take these and have a look around. Let them guide you. Let me know if you see anything interesting."

Grey delicately took hold of the all-seeing glasses. She expected the weight of the world. They were light as a feather. She gently placed them on her face and looked out the window. She could see the path before her. "I see it," she confirmed excitedly. "Or them, rather. They're tall, but they don't look like the pines. They don't even look like trees."

"They're definitely not trees," Bo laughed. "They may scrape the sky like Mrs. Pine, with just as much attitude, but you're not looking at the country anymore. You're seeing high-rises, which are tall buildings in cities. They're built to rise above all the other buildings. That's where a few of the Black Mountain Farm weekend guests live."

Grey laughed out loud. *What a play on words,* she thought to herself. She had literally seen that writing on the wall. Aim high, rise above. Totally different time and context, but as Bo liked to point out, it was all relative.

"High-rise, huh? Well played. What and where are they?" Grey asked.

"This is what some homes look like in the city," Bo explained. "While Mr. Joe and Miss B's house spreads out horizontally, these homes are designed to spread out vertically. Each home sits on top of the next, all the way up to the sky."

Grey stared at the buildings. They looked like stacks of tree houses, or rather, glass houses. She thought for a minute.

"Are the glass houses in the city built with the same intention as Lone Star Lodge?" she asked.

"Not all of them," Bo sighed. "Unfortunately, it's a different world out there."

A lightbulb went off in Grey's mind. "Miss Jay

once told me that sometimes an animal crosses paths with a human. Sometimes they're destined to meet. Meeting my forever human has always been my secret dream. It's what I've always wanted. I've asked for it so many times, hoping to will it into existence. That's my human's home, isn't it? In that high-rise? The one that's glowing?"

Bo watched Grey as the full picture emerged.

Grey then pointed to a trail on the mountain as the glasses shifted. "And that's clearly the path I take to get started. They have the same glow."

Bo remained quiet. This was Grey's meeting with destiny.

They sat together in silence as Grey collected her thoughts.

"Isn't it crazy that I came to the Lodge determined to find a way to remain here at the farm?" Grey pondered. "That's all I could see the whole way up. Staying on the farm was all I could think about, even though I wanted more than life in the Jam Barn and I knew I wasn't supposed to stay there. I just didn't want someone else to take away my spot. I didn't want it to be on anyone else's terms. Now that I know the choice is mine, I know I'm supposed to be there, in the city . . . at least for now." Grey pointed to the glowing high-rise.

Grey paused and looked at Bo, who was now leaning forward, absorbing her every word.

How the tables had turned.

"You want to know the funny part?" Grey asked, though it was a rhetorical question. "I knew that I was a gift to Dawn, but I just realized Dawn was a gift to me, too. Without her, and without this whole journey, I wouldn't be sitting here looking at my new home."

"Everything happens for a reason," Bo smiled.

"Yeah, but the universe has a twisted sense of humor," Grey countered.

"And that's life," Bo concluded with the dramatic flair of someone who'd just played the winning card.

65

Chapter Sixty-Five
The Interview

The mystery of the room with the paper and pens had been solved. The purple door led to the writing room at *The Buzzy Bark.* It all made sense to Grey now.

"So, the papers, the lobipens, the tables . . . " Grey trailed off as she listed the items she had used to practice her power in the room where she'd discovered her magical voice.

"Yes, that's where Mrs. Pine oversees stories and layouts for the weekly paper," Bo confirmed. "There's also a branch outside that shoots broadcasts and breaks exclusive stories to the BMF community. Mrs. Pine was hoping, or rather planning, for an interview with you. Laura is standing by to share your story, but she can only report *your* words. Your truth. That was our deal.

"Mrs. Pine and I created a space that gave me her height, providing me with the view I needed to see the best in animals. Mrs. Pine guaranteed editorial integrity in exchange. She can only report the story as you remember it. That's how she honors our guests. This is your tale, after all. Your opportunity to tell it the way you saw it."

"Do you know what Laura's going to ask me?" Grey inquired.

"Does it matter?" Bo laughed. "They're your answers. Are you ready?"

Grey was ready. Surprisingly ready. She stood, smiled, and walked from the green room to the purple door. It was open this time. She followed the same path through the room, but this time it led her to a group of bees standing by a branch outside.

"Right this way," one of the bees directed her.

Grey saw Laura sitting next to an empty chair. She was surrounded by a crew of busy bees. Laura motioned for Grey to take a seat. The crew made quick adjustments and ran a few tests to ensure Grey's voice was coming in clearly. She felt surprisingly calm and completely at ease with her surroundings. She realized this had been the plan all along.

Grey sat up straight. She saw the glow of the red light counting down, advising Laura that it was time. This red light didn't bother Grey.

"Thank you for joining me. I'm Laura, Special Reporter for *The Buzzy Bark.* We're live from Black Mountain Farm, where we've been working behind the scenes to bring you the exclusive story of 'Grey: The Barn Cat with a Gift at BMF.'"

As they made it through her story, Grey found her groove.

"Tell us: where do you go from here?" Laura led. Grey almost laughed out loud at the final question of the interview.

"Well, I think we both know I'll need to choose my words carefully," Grey joked. Laura and the crew laughed. "Here's what I can tell you for sure: I will continue to aim high, rise above, and pave the way for others to follow."

66

Chapter Sixty-Six
Code of Honor

Grey left the interview and went straight to Miss Jay.

Grey had seen her path through the all-seeing glasses, and she wanted her guardian and friend to hear about it before anyone else. She'd been as vague as she could when Laura asked about her next steps. It came as no real surprise to either of them that Miss Jay already had a hunch before Grey said it out loud.

"When we were playing the Hoo Game, the first thing that came to my mind was humans," Grey revealed. "Humans make me happy. I'm ready to meet my person and explore a new place for a while."

Miss Jay smiled. "I know," she said without hesitation. "It's time for you to find the human you were destined to meet and plant some roots of your own."

"It's my choice to leave the mountain, and it will honor my happiness," Grey continued. "I just wish I could honor both of us at the same time. I want to thank you, Miss Jay. I wouldn't be here without you."

Miss Jay placed her wings on Grey's shoulders to emphasize her next point. "You've already honored me," Miss Jay replied, unable to contain her emotion. "It's your time to shine. Follow your light. Or as Estelle would say: earn those beautiful stripes and enjoy the ride."

Chapter Sixty-Seven
The Road Ahead

Grey watched as Bo triple-checked everything for their journey back, from Biggie's Wipi cup to the warm sunlight and the breeze. She wondered if Bo always acted this way when his guests left the Lodge. Bo looked like a proud parent sending his kids off into the world.

Grey laughed as Elaine, all sass, landed on Bo's

shoulders. "Um, h-e-l-l-o?" she flapped, tickling the serious owl until he couldn't help but flinch. "Don't I have a role in this? I dare say I'm the best guide for the kind of path she's taking."

"Of course, Elaine," Bo confirmed. "I'm hoping you'll help Grey gauge the pace today. We all know there's no one better equipped at feeling out change than a butterfly."

Bo motioned for Grey, Biggie, Miss Jay, and Elaine to follow him to the gate. As the gate opened, Bo hugged Grey and whispered in her ear, "If you need me, motion for me. It's that simple. Remember, the glasses see all. The trail is clear today. Nothing but wildflowers and blue skies ahead."

"You're leading this dance, darlin'," Biggie checked in with Grey as they crossed over the line of the Lodge. "Where to?"

"We're taking Gwendolyn Lane to the back gate," Grey instructed.

What a difference a few days made. The group walked with ease. They strolled with a lighthearted air, stepping to the rhythm of old friends. They laughed together as they rehashed memories to pass the time. Biggie talked about the trails he used to run, and Miss Jay shared stories about the different animals she met growing up.

Elaine explained her transformation from a caterpillar to a butterfly, and how her first flight had felt so liberating. The air was pure and the day full of promise.

Grey heard the sound before she saw the lights ahead. It was the car of a weekend guest on their way back to the city. This was her person. She could feel it. “Biggie, stop,” she directed her dear friend. “That’s my new ride.”

Grey jumped out of the Wipi cup that had carried and protected her until this point. She faced her friends. She could feel herself glowing, and she could see that glow in their eyes. Elaine bounced up and down with excitement.

“Remember, life always comes full circle,” Miss Jay smiled.

“I know, Miss Jay,” Grey grinned. “I’ll see you again. Don’t let Biggie eat too many berries on the way back down. I hear he’s trying to shake off a few pounds, for the ladies.”

Grey turned and ran toward her new ride. As she gained speed, she yelled, “Break it!” Her words flew ahead of her. They broke the fence in front of the gate, creating a small opening just large enough for her to run straight through.

Biggie and Miss Jay watched as the pieces of fence fell to the ground, clearing the way for Grey to position herself on the grass ahead of her ride. As the universe predicted, the car stopped to let in its new passenger. Grey was going home.

"How about that? A barn cat with a gift," Biggie laughed.

"She always did enjoy breaking the rules." Miss Jay smirked.

Life always
comes full circle.

Encore

Saw the tablet today, told my story my way;
Read the headlines of great expectations to come.
Fought the order of time, with the flip of a crime;
Watched my words warrant hope
and our battles were won.

To home I go, my path before me;
To home I go, his glasses helped see.
From the widow entwined, many miles behind,
And our hearts ring true.

So, I rode on his rack, a sentimental deer track
On the way to my high-rise above in the sky.
Felt the car speed ahead, prepare for my new bed;
Looking out at the stretch between here and homestead.

To home I go, my path before me;
To home I go, his glasses helped see.
From arrogance of mind, we immerse in kind,
And our hearts ring true.

Now I rest on my perch, to the drumbeat of rain;
Spend my hours in vain looking down memory lane.
See the city unfold, with new stars in the mold;
Earn my stripes, learn new beats, and laugh every day.

To home I go, my path before me,
To home I go, his glasses helped see.
With the stars aligned, my destiny defined,
And our hearts ring true.

Acknowledgments

My dream has always been to write a book. Not just any book. I wanted it to stand for something. So, I waited for the moment to present itself. There was something about this goal in particular that told me to have faith. Moreover, it told me to have a purpose. Everything happens for a reason, and my journey as an author needed to be intentional. *The Land of the Pines*, which marks the beginning of the Loodor Tales series, was worth the wait. It would not have been possible without the support of many along the way. My endless gratitude goes to the following:

To my family for their unwavering support, inspiration, and feedback. Special thanks to my mother, Lou. Without you, none of this would have been possible. Same goes for "Double Trouble"!

To my friends for their ongoing encouragement and unconditional love. Special thanks to my lifelong friend, Marnie. You've always held me accountable to the goals I set out to achieve. Your inner strength has been a driving force in helping me realize my dreams.

To George D. Hamilton for his guidance in building the foundation from which to give back.

To Holly Mason at LINQ, my partner in all things purpose driven.

To Milli Brown and the Brown Books Publishing Group team for seeing the creative vision in my story and understanding how important this book is to me.

Mr. and Mrs. Pine, Grey, Miss Jay, Dawn, Biggie, Elaine, and Bo: we all thank you.

About the Author
Summer Nilsson

A seasoned CEO, entrepreneur, consultant, and marketing veteran, over the course of her career Summer Nilsson has represented the biggest names in publishing, fashion, and the arts, including *People*, *Food Network Magazine*, *House Beautiful*, *Who What Wear*, among many others. She is the founder and CEO of Loodor and author of *The Land of the Pines.*

Loodor is built on the belief that life always comes full circle. We entertain with premium content that invokes thought, inspires communication, and fuels creativity. Through storytelling, products, and purpose-driven partnerships, we strive to spread a message of positivity, reinforce kindness, and underscore the power of one's voice, beginning with the first tale, *The Land of the Pines.*

Raised in the small East Texas town of Daingerfield, Summer developed a deep appreciation for animals and nature. Though her career eventually led her to the city, her heart never left her hometown roots. The fictional Grey of the Loodor Tales was based upon Summer's own cat, rescued at five weeks old from the side of a rural road on a visit to her hometown in East Texas. The real-life Grey inspired Summer to establish the Nilsson Open A Dor Foundation, which aims to support organizations working to place sheltered animals in forever homes.

Summer lives in Dallas, Texas.

About the Illustrator

Blayne Fox

Midwestern resident Blayne Fox grew up romping through the Missouri woodlands, letting her imagination take flight to create magical kingdoms and creatures wherever she went. Predominantly self-taught, Blayne knew what she was going to be from a very young age: an artist. After attending art college, she plunged into her industry, working for clients such as *Discovery Channel* and *National Geographic Kids* within her first year out of school. She is now represented by Deborah Wolfe Ltd and primarily focuses on illustrating children's books and graphic novels.